UNDER
STRI

Dyan Sheldon is a children's author, adult novelist and humorist. Her books include the novels *And Baby Makes Two*; *Tall, Thin and Blonde*; *Ride On, Sister Vincent*; *The Boy of My Dreams*; *Confessions of a Teenage Drama Queen*; and *Undercover Angel*, prequel to *Undercover Angel Strikes Again*. She has also written stories about Harry and Chicken, *Leon Loves Bugs*, *Lizzie and Charley Go Shopping* and several picture books including *The Whales' Song* (Winner of the 1991 Kate Greenaway Medal). American by birth, Dyan Sheldon lives in north London.

Books by the same author

Elena the Frog
Harry and Chicken
Harry the Explorer
Harry's Holiday
He's Not My Dog
Leon Loves Bugs
Lizzie and Charley Go Shopping
Undercover Angel
Ride On, Sister Vincent

For older readers

The Boy of My Dreams
Tall, Thin and Blonde
*Confessions of a Teenage
Drama Queen*
And Baby Makes Two

UNDERCOVER ANGEL STRIKES AGAIN

DYAN SHELDON

WALKER BOOKS
AND SUBSIDIARIES
LONDON · BOSTON · SYDNEY

For Chiqui –
for obvious reasons

First published 2001 by Walker Books Ltd
87 Vauxhall Walk, London SE11 5HJ

2 4 6 8 10 9 7 5 3 1

Text © 2001 Dyan Sheldon
Cover illustration © 2001 Spike Gerrell

This book has been typeset in Sabon

Printed in Great Britain by Cox & Wyman Ltd, Reading, Berkshire

British Library Cataloguing in Publication Data:
a catalogue record for this book is
available from the British Library

ISBN 0-7445-5952-9

CONTENTS

1   Kuba Bamber Rocks My Boat   7

2   I Make a Decision Based on Fear   13

3   I Give an Academy
Award Winning Performance   21

4   I Discover That Everyone
Has a Price   27

5   Bomb Voyage   38

6   Welcome to Wyndach   49

7   Night One and Counting   59

8   The Educational Part of
Our Trip Begins   76

9   War at Wyndach   89

10   Laughing Last   98

KUBA BAMBER
ROCKS MY BOAT

Mr Palfry, our science teacher, was talking about the class trip.

"We'll be visiting a region rich in history," Mr Palfry was saying. "There have been human settlements there for thousands of years. Stone Age ... Iron Age ... Roman..."

He sounded almost breathless, as though this was all incredibly exciting. But believe me when I say that it wasn't. It was about as exciting as eating dry oats. If we'd been going somewhere that was rich in fun, like Disneyland Paris, it would have been exciting. But we weren't going to Disneyland Paris – we were going to some mountain in Wales. I had to struggle to keep my eyes open.

I wasn't the only one. Most of the class had started nodding off the minute Mr Palfry said "rich in history". The only exceptions were Kuba Bamber and Archie Spongo. Both Kuba and Archie were new to the country and the school, which probably had something to do with their ability to stay awake during Mr Palfry's pep talk. Archie's English wasn't great, so he always paid attention in class, but Kuba, whose English was better than mine, always paid attention because she was a model student.

And then Mr Palfry got to what he obviously thought was the best part.

"Not only have there been settlements at Wyndach for thousands of years," he gushed, "but it's an unspoilt wilderness that will give us the rare opportunity to study some of the indigenous flora and fauna that are sadly gone from much of the British Isles."

Archie Spongo raised his hand.

Mr Palfry raised an eyebrow. He seemed surprised to discover that someone other than Kuba was still awake.

"Yes, Archie?"

Archie smiled. Archie always smiled when he was nervous. He smiled most of the time.

"Excuse me, Mr Palfry," said Archie. He had a heavy accent that made it sound as if he was talking through a mouthful of wet bread. "But what does 'indigenous' mean? Is it like a disease?"

Eddie Kilgour woke up first. He started gasping with laughter, and then almost everybody else joined in.

"No, Archie," said Mr Palfry loudly. "No, it isn't a disease. Would someone like to tell Archie what 'indigenous' means?" His eyes moved round the room and stopped. "Eddie?"

Behind me Kuba finally laughed, and it was definitely *at* Eddie, not *with* him.

Eddie looked over and glowered. But it wasn't Kuba he was glowering at, of course. It was me. Kuba was not only a model student, she was also sweet and shy. Even Eddie thought she was a total angel. It would never occur to him that Kuba would laugh at him like that; so it had to be me.

That sort of thing had been happening a lot lately. It happened in science, it happened in English, it happened in maths, it happened in the playground, it happened in the cafeteria. If there was the slightest chance of getting Eddie in trouble, someone did. But even though that someone was always Kuba, she always made it look as if that someone was me.

I turned round to do a little glowering of my own in Kuba's direction. She didn't so much as blink. Maybe I'm slow, but it was the first time I realized that she was doing it on purpose. For some reason Kuba Bamber was deliberately rocking my boat.

"Eddie?" prompted Mr Palfry. "Eddie, can you explain to Archie what 'indigenous' means?"

Eddie didn't know. He didn't say he didn't

9

know, of course; he just frowned as though he was trying to come up with an explanation that was simple enough for Archie Spongo to understand. His best mate, Mark, didn't know either. Mark was looking blank and trying not to grin. Eddie glared at me again as if it was all my fault.

The last thing I wanted was for Eddie Kilgour to be angry with me. I'd always been considered a little different by my schoolmates, but my stock had risen considerably since the Battle of Campton. After I stopped Mr Bamber's bulldozers from levelling the woods so he could build a housing development and a golf course, I was famous for a while. I even had my picture in the paper with the caption CHILD LEADS THE WAY TO A GREENER FUTURE, and a clip on the news showed me lying down in front of a bulldozer, holding up a placard. My mother, the environmental activist, was so proud of me that she broke at least three of her most cherished principles and bought me the Nike sweatshirt I'd longed for as a reward. With my new fame and my new sweatshirt the rest of the class had finally accepted me as human. Even Eddie had stopped tormenting me all the time. And I wanted to keep it like that.

I put up my hand. Because my mother's both a gardener and an environmental activist, "indigenous" is one word I know well. Before

I could tie my own shoes I'd been taught that McDonald's is *not* indigenous to Great Britain, that the holly bush *is* indigenous to Great Britain, and that the mouse-eared bat used to be.

"Indigenous means *native*!" I called out.

Kuba jabbed me with her pencil.

"Thank you, Elmo," said Mr Palfry. He didn't sound as thankful as I'd expected. He peered at Archie over his glasses. "Do you understand that, Archie? Indigenous means *native*." He smiled gamely. "To a place," he explained. "Native to a place."

Archie Spongo kept grinning in a non-committal sort of way.

"You know!" spluttered Eddie. "Like *you're* native to the planet Weirdo."

This remark had the desired effect. The boys who weren't killing themselves laughing started humming the theme tune to *The Twilight Zone*.

Mark leaned towards Archie and whispered loudly and ghoulishly, "In space, no one can hear you scream..."

The laughter doubled.

Mr Palfry rapped on his desk.

"Did you have something you wanted to share with the rest of the class, Eddie?" asked Mr Palfry.

But Eddie was a professional when it came to this sort of thing. He should have been –

he'd been doing it since primary school. Teacher interference never slowed him down for long.

He gazed back at Mr Palfry with the serious, earnest expression of someone questing for knowledge.

"I was just wondering if there are natives where Archie comes from," said Eddie. "You know, who paint themselves blue and worship the moon and stuff like that."

"Eddie," said Mr Palfry, with what I thought was incredible patience. "Eddie, the last place Archie lived was London. Remember?"

This was hard to believe, considering the way Archie talked and dressed, but it was true. Archie Spongo had lived in London before he came to Campton, but he'd lived somewhere else before that. Somewhere where they were dropping bombs and the electricity never worked.

"I'm sure there are people who paint themselves blue and worship the moon in London," Mr Palfry went on, "but I doubt if they run around in loin cloths with spears in their hands, if that's what you had in mind."

Eddie pretended to be embarrassed. He slapped his forehead, and groaned, and made faces. His audience spluttered in appreciation.

"Of course!" cried Eddie. He gave Mr Palfry a big cheesy grin. "How could I be so stupid?"

I MAKE A DECISION
BASED ON FEAR

"I don't believe you, Elmo Blue," said Kuba as we went to lunch. She swung her book bag over her shoulder and slammed me in the arm. "You really are too much sometimes."

"Me?" I was flabbergasted. "*I'm* too much? What'd I do?"

The book bag whopped me again. "You bailed Eddie out, that's what you did. Why can't you ever just leave well alone?"

She could talk. The fastest way to get Kuba to do something was to tell her not to.

"Me? Excuse me ... you're the one who nearly got me in trouble with Eddie." I gave her a sour look. "Again." My look became accusing. "Don't think I haven't noticed how you're always provoking him and making it look like it's me," I went on. "Because I have, and I'm getting pretty fed up with it."

"I hope you're not threatening me," said

Kuba sweetly. "It isn't something that I'd recommend."

If anyone else had heard her, they would have thought she was joking. At school Kuba acts like she's about as hard as custard. Which is ironic, really, since she's the last person you'd ever want to mess with.

The important thing you have to know about Kuba is that she not only behaves like an angel – she really is an angel. She's an undercover angel, disguised as an orphan from South America. She doesn't have wings, but she does have a halo. It's not a circle of light the way they are in old paintings, though; it's a haze of blue over her head. I'm the only one who can see it, but she wears an old hat to cover it, just in case. Kuba claims she came to Campton to help people, but in my opinion the real reason she came was to bother me.

"I'm not threatening you," I said irritably. "I'm just mentioning something you seem to have overlooked."

Kuba, of course, continued to overlook it.

"Eddie was about to make a complete fool of himself," she informed me. "And *you* saved him."

"That's not the point," I protested. "The point is that you keep setting me up. And anyway, I didn't *save* him. I just happened to know the answer. Since when is it a crime to answer a question?"

14

"Even Mr Palfry was annoyed with you," said Kuba, and she opened the door to the cafeteria and strode through.

I walked straight into her because instead of striding on into the dining room she stopped at the door.

"Talk of the devil," she muttered half under her breath.

Eddie Kilgour and Mark Crother were sitting with some other boys at a table near the drinks machine. Archie Spongo was at the table in front of Eddie's with some other kids no one else wanted to sit with.

I watched Archie for a few seconds, sitting there in the wrong clothes and the wrong haircut. He looked like a pelican set down in a flock of parrots. Or a sitting duck.

And then I noticed something else. Archie didn't know it, but Eddie was copying everything he did. If Archie scratched his head, Eddie scratched his head. If Archie unpacked his lunch, Eddie pretended to unpack his lunch too. I know it doesn't sound that thrilling, but it was keeping Eddie's table pretty amused.

"So," said Kuba. "I suppose we'd better find some seats."

I could tell she meant her and me. "We? Where's Ariel today?"

Kuba usually had lunch with Ariel Moordock and I sat with Carl and Jamal.

"She had to go somewhere with her

mother," said Kuba vaguely. "To the optician's, I think."

That suited me fine. Carl and Jamal were all right, but we weren't great mates. The only reason I sat with them was because they'd asked me to share a room with them on the class trip, and the only reason they asked me to share a room with them was so they weren't the ones who got stuck with Archie Spongo.

"OK." I pointed right. "Let's sit over there." Which was about as far away as we could get from Eddie and his mates and still be in the room.

Kuba didn't budge. "Somebody should do something about them," she mumbled to herself. "They're getting out of control."

Her eyes were on Eddie and Mark, who were nearly choking over Eddie's impersonation of Archie trying to get his juice carton open, so I pretended I hadn't heard her. If anybody was going to do something about Eddie and Mark, it definitely wasn't going to be me.

"Come on." I gave her arm a tug. "Let's sit down."

Kuba treated me to her sweetest smile. "Your table's just been taken." She pointed left. "We'll have to sit over there."

And she sailed off to the corner where Archie Spongo was inspiring Eddie Kilgour to new comic heights.

Even though I hate sitting by myself at

lunch, I would have if it hadn't been for the fact that Kuba was right – as usual. All of a sudden there wasn't anywhere else to sit. It was like a reverse miracle. I took a deep breath and followed my best friend into the darkest corner of the cafeteria.

There were a couple of kids sitting at the table behind Eddie, but they suddenly got up and left as we approached.

"You see," said Kuba. "Perfect."

Perfect for what? I felt like asking. *Suicide?* To my relief, neither Eddie nor any of the others seemed to notice us sit down. They probably couldn't see through the tears of laughter.

I opened the brown paper bag that contained my lunch and Kuba opened the trendy chrome box that held hers.

"What have you got?" I spoke softly. If they didn't know we were there, I wasn't going to tell them.

Kuba said "What?" as Eddie and his mates let out a laugh that shook our table.

Kuba frowned. Tiny flecks of gold glinted in her eyes. Experience has taught me that the gold glints in Kuba Bamber's eyes are usually a bad sign.

"What have you got?" I repeated. "I've got nut cutlet sandwiches and vegetable sticks." My mother's got a thing about healthy eating.

"Soup and pasta salad," said Kuba. Mrs

17

Bamber has a thing about the posh deli in town.

Kuba was taking her brushed-steel Thermos out of the box when Eddie tapped Archie Spongo on the shoulder. She had her back to them, but I could tell from the way the gold in her eyes got darker that she knew exactly what was happening.

I tried not to pay any attention to what Eddie Kilgour was doing. What did I care, as long as he wasn't doing it to me?

"Soup," I said wistfully. I never brought soup any more because my Thermos had a picture of Snoopy on it. "That sounds good."

Which was more or less what Eddie was saying at that very second.

"Doesn't that look good..." Eddie was saying.

Kuba slowly took the lid off her flask.

Eddie reached out and snatched Archie's sandwich from him with one flick of the wrist. "Look what Spongo's got for lunch!" He held the wedge of white bread and something pink in the air. "Doesn't that look *good*?"

There was a chorus of "Yum ... yum..." from his table.

Mark did his pig impersonation. "Looks like pork," he said.

Eddie shook his head thoughtfully. "I'm not sure. It looks more like roast rat to me."

Archie made a grab for Eddie's hand. "Give

me back my sandwich, please."

Eddie turned so the sandwich was out of his reach. "What do you think, Mark?" Eddie lifted the top slice of bread. "Doesn't this look like roast rat to you?"

Very, very slowly, Kuba poured some soup into the lid of her Thermos. She seemed to be a million miles away. That was OK with me because I was having trouble keeping up my end of the conversation. I really didn't want to know what Eddie was doing, but I was fascinated. It was like watching the Godfather at work.

"I'm going to get a drink," said Kuba suddenly. "Do you want anything?"

I must have been paying more attention to Eddie than I thought, because I hadn't even seen her get up.

I shook my head.

Mark took a slice of pink stuff from the bread and held it between his fingertips. He turned it this way and that. "You know," he said. "I think it is rat."

Somebody made a gagging sound.

"Gross!" said Eddie. "Spongo eats rat! Get that stuff away from me."

He shoved Mark's hand and the slice of luncheon meat went flying. It landed on one of the other boys, who hurled it back across the table. It hit Archie on the head.

Archie was trying really hard not to cry as

he removed the meat from his hair and watched the rest of his lunch soar through the air, but it wasn't working all that well. His eyes were starting to glisten.

That's when the table started to quiver. I didn't notice at first, not until Kuba's Thermos started to vibrate. I looked down at the table. It was quivering so much that I thought it was going for lift-off.

In the end, though, it wasn't the table that took off – it was Kuba's flask. It shot into the air like a tiny rocket, hung there for a few seconds, spraying liquid like a fountain, and then it drifted back down without so much as a bump.

Suddenly Eddie and his mates were all shrieking and jumping up and down, dripping Mrs Bamber's gourmet soup all over the floor.

Eddie's eyes met mine.

"Good grief," said Kuba, reappearing with a carton of apple juice in her hand. She looked concerned. "Whatever happened?"

"Why don't you ask Elmo?" snarled Eddie.

And that's when I decided that I wasn't going on the class trip. Not for anything.

I GIVE AN ACADEMY AWARD WINNING PERFORMANCE

I waited till the last minute before pulling out of the trip. There was a very good reason for this caution: my mother.

My mother is a woman of many principles. If I'd given her the slightest hint that any bullying was going on, she'd have been up at the school faster than an electron. And that was the last thing I wanted. What you want when somebody is pushing you around is to turn into a superhero, not have your mother intervening. It only makes things worse. Archie Spongo's aunt had been to see the head three times since Archie started at Campton, but instead of chilling Eddie and Mark out, it had only made them more determined.

I was drawn and quiet when I got home from school the afternoon before the trip, but nobody noticed, of course. My mother was out spreading cow dung round someone's garden, my dad was working on one of his fountains and my grandparents had my baby sister Gertie with them in their studio because they were giving their Latin dance lesson and Gertie loves to salsa.

Nobody noticed how drawn and quiet I was later, when we were getting supper ready. They were all talking and laughing while I sat at the table, tearing lettuce like someone whose bones have dissolved. The only person who said anything to me was my Uncle Cal.

"Shake a leg there, Elmo," said Cal. "Your mother can grow lettuce faster than you shred it."

Nobody noticed how drawn and quiet I was at supper either. Normal families eat their meals in front of the telly and only speak if they want the salt or something, but my family sit at a table and everyone competes for air space all the time. It wasn't until I'd spilled half my water on my pasta that anyone even remembered I was there. Some of the water splashed on my mother. She removed Gertie's fist from her salad and looked over at me at last.

"Are you all right, Elmo?" asked my mother. She was studying me as if I might have leaf mould. "You've hardly touched your food."

Trembling slightly, I put the glass back on the table and slowly lifted my head.

"Yeah…" My voïce was weak and low. "No … I'm sorry…" My eyes narrowed with pain. "I'm not feeling very well."

My grandmother broke off the argument she was having with my grandfather to clap a palm to my forehead. Breadcrumbs trickled down my face.

"He hasn't got a temperature," she informed my mother.

I moaned feebly. "I must have. I'm burning up inside." I gazed at her with the dazed expression of someone whose temperature is high enough to cook an egg. "The hand method isn't exactly scientific, is it?" I suggested gently.

My mother removed Gertie's fist from her potatoes.

"No, but it works," said my mother. She doesn't care about things being scientific, and she hasn't trusted thermometers since she realized they can be heated on a light bulb.

"Maybe it's that flu that's going around," suggested my grandfather, joint owner of Blues' School of International Dance. "Half the Latin class were away."

My grandmother was peering into my face. "You do look a bit peaky. Maybe you need more exercise."

My grandmother thinks everybody needs more exercise – preferably ballroom dancing.

"I don't think I can even walk," I whispered.

"I actually feel a little faint."

My Uncle Cal and my Aunt Lucy, who describe themselves as "wall artists" (which means they never paint a picture smaller than the size of a lorry), interrupted the conversation they were having on whether or not Cal should get his lip pierced to say in horrified unison, "Paint? It can't be our paint. Our paint is non-toxic."

"Not *paint*," I croaked. "*Faint*. I feel like I'm going to faint."

"Tell me exactly where it hurts, Elmo," said my mother. "Your head? Your throat? Your stomach?"

"Everywhere," I whispered. "Even my hair hurts." I pushed my plate away. "Maybe I'd better just go to bed. I don't think I've even got the strength to get undressed."

My father, as usual, had been doodling fountain designs on a piece of paper, but now he joined the conversation too.

"What about the class trip?" asked my father. "Isn't that soon?"

"Yeah," I croaked. "Tomorrow. Eight a.m. sharp." I groaned in misery. "I feel so awful, I completely forgot about the trip." I took a deep breath and tried to sit up straight. I winced in agony.

My mother was disentangling Gertie's hand from her hair and didn't say anything, but my grandmother gallantly filled in for her.

"Oh, there's no way you can go when you feel like this." I assumed she was speaking to me, but she was looking at my grandfather. "Remember that time in Venice, Monrose? When you insisted on dancing even though you had that bug?"

My grandfather smiled fondly at the memory. "Brought down two waiters, four tables and the dessert trolley."

My mother looked as concerned as a woman with a two-year-old attached to her head can look, which isn't that concerned.

"Maybe you'll feel better in the morning," she said. "After you've had a good night's sleep." She can have a very sly smile when she wants, Grace Blue. "After all, I know how much you've been looking forward to the trip."

She was being sarcastic. My mother thought the idea of roughing it in Wales was brilliant because there was plenty of vegetation and no modern conveniences or souvenirs, but she knew I would have preferred Disneyland.

"I was…" I lied. "I am." I flinched with the effort of trying to speak. "I've got to go on the trip." I winced again, for effect. "Maybe I will feel better in the morning." To prove how much better I was going to feel in the morning, I tried to get to my feet. But I was too weak and unwell; I collapsed back in my chair.

My mother gave me a sympathetic smile.

"Don't worry. If you do miss the trip, I'll take you to see that battery farm I was telling you about when you're feeling better. Make it up to you."

At this rate I could be sick for a really long time.

My room's right at the top of the house. It's the smallest room, but it's also the most private. Once I got to the first floor and couldn't be heard in the kitchen, I took the stairs two at a time, humming a happy song under my breath. I'd done it! I opened the door to my room.

I froze. All was not as it should have been in the room of Elmo Blue. Everything looked the way it had earlier – my shelves of books, my bed and bedside table, my desk and my computer, the newspaper photograph of Bill Gates, my hero and role model, that I'd taped to the wall – but there was one significant change.

Kuba Bamber was sitting at my desk with her back to me, blasting blue monsters into oblivion on my computer. She didn't turn round.

I DISCOVER
THAT EVERYONE
HAS A PRICE

Unfortunately, there isn't anything unusual in finding Kuba Bamber in my room, using my computer and trying to reorganize my life, when she should be across the road watching telly with the Bambers. Kuba has been appearing in my room, uninvited and largely unwanted, since the day I met her. This seems to be typical behaviour for angels.

"Go home," I ordered. "I've got flu. I need to rest."

Kuba squinted at the monitor as she blitzed a mob of shaggy creatures with glowing red eyes.

"What you need to do is pack," Kuba corrected me. "You haven't even started yet. The bus leaves at eight, remember."

I threw myself on my bed and kicked off my vegan-friendly canvas trainers with a sigh.

"Let it leave." My face looked anguished

with pain and fever. I smiled inwardly. "I'm not going. I'm too sick."

Clickclickclickclickclick ... blue monsters evaporated from the screen in puffs of green smoke at a rate of knots.

"The right word is *ill*," said Kuba. "And you're not. You're faking it."

I've discovered that there are a lot of things people assume about angels that aren't true. You know, that they're very kind and patient and delicate, stuff like that. But there is one thing people assume about angels that *is* true: they're hard to fool. I, for one, am happy my mother is not an angel, I'll tell you that.

"All right, so I'm not *that* ill," I conceded. "But I'm still not going on the trip."

"Yes, you are." Kuba leaned towards the monitor. "I'm only going because you're going. And besides, you said you'd share with Carl and Jamal. You can't pull out now."

"Oh yes I can. Carl and Jamal will find someone else, and you've got Ariel to hang out with." I was determined: wild BMWs wouldn't get me on that trip.

"Ariel's not *you*," said Kuba. "And make sure you pack your rain gear. It may get stormy."

"What are you, deaf?" I stared at the back of her head. "I'm not going, Kuba. Everything's been OK between me and Eddie since the bulldozers, and I want to keep it that way.

Stop rocking my boat. I don't want to go."

"*Everything's been OK between me and Eddie*," mimicked Kuba, making faces at the screen. "That's typical of you, isn't it, Elmo? You think only of yourself."

"Well, *you* certainly don't think of me," I snapped back. "You sprayed that soup all over Eddie, and then you made it look as if I did it."

"I didn't make it look anything," said Kuba primly. "Eddie jumped to his own conclusions."

"Yeah, well, if I'm not around he won't be able to jump to anything, will he? Because if you think I'm going to the wilderness with the two of you, you'd better think again. I know you, Kuba Bamber – for some twisted reason you're determined to ruin my life."

"*I'm* ruining *your* life?" Kuba swivelled round in my chair. She's fairly good at snorting with derision. "You really do delude yourself, don't you, Elmo?" she demanded. "If you were a little more objective, you'd see that you've been behaving pretty weirdly lately." She scowled at the large white tick on my chest. "You and your stupid sweatshirt. You were making real progress, and now you're backsliding again. You stood up to Mr Bamber and his golf course, but the minute you see Eddie and Mark you turn to jelly."

"I didn't stand up to the bulldozers," I corrected her. "I sat down." I picked up my book from the bedside table and ducked behind it. "And if you really want to know why I don't stand up to Eddie, it's because Eddie and I have a history."

"Oh?" I could feel Kuba looking at me. "What sort of a history?"

I turned a page. "It's a bit like the history between the white men and the Indians of the Americas."

"Let me guess which you are," said Kuba.

"He pushed me around all through primary school," I said from behind my book. I felt sorry for Archie, I really did, but I couldn't help being relieved that Eddie was pushing someone else around for a change.

"So why did he pick on you?" probed Kuba. "What did you do?"

I'd never told anyone about what happened, and I certainly had no intention of telling Kuba Bamber, but my mouth didn't get the message from my brain.

"I wore my Womble slippers to school."

"What?"

I said it a little louder this time. "I wore my Womble slippers to school."

My Womble slippers were my favourite possession when I was little. I was so proud of them that I asked my mother if I could wear them to school. A normal mother who eats meat and takes her son to McDonald's would have known that this was a really bad idea, but

30

my mother thought it was brilliant. I wore my slippers to school. They caused quite a sensation. It was Eddie Kilgour who started singing "Remember you're a Womble", and it became my theme tune for the next five years.

By the time I had finished my tragic tale, my best friend was clutching her sides because she was laughing so much.

I glared at her over the top of my book. "It isn't that funny," I said sourly.

"Oh, I don't know." She wiped a tear from her eye. "Look on the bright side, Elmo," said Kuba. "Maybe Bill Gates had a similar experience when he was little."

"I don't care if Bill went to school in his Mickey Mouse pyjamas." I turned back to the page I was on, even though I hadn't read a single word. "I'm not going on the trip, and that's final. Maybe I'd risk it if we were going to Disneyland Paris, but not Wales. Wales is dead boring if you ask me."

"Well, what do you know?" said Kuba. "Eddie and Mark agree with you."

I should have ignored that last statement. It was meant to make me curious. It was meant to make me look over.

I was curious. I looked over. There were no more blue monsters on the screen. I was powerless to resist. Against my will, my body rose from the bed.

I could hear Mark Crother's voice coming

from my computer's speakers.

"My cousin's class went skiing for their class trip," Mark was saying. "In Switzerland. They had a brilliant time."

"My sister went to Barcelona," said Eddie. "Even Barcelona's better than Wales."

I stood behind Kuba, staring at the monitor. Eddie and Mark were sitting on the floor of Eddie's room. There were two cans and a bowl of crisps between them. I knew it was Eddie's room because of the football posters. Eddie's mad keen on football. I'm not. I'm not really a physical sort of person. Like Bill Gates, I'm more a mental sort of person. It's another thing Eddie's always held against me.

Mark sighed. "We're going to be bored out of our brains."

"As if they have any," mumbled Kuba.

Eddie picked up a can and took a sip. "Oh, I don't know," he purred. "It doesn't have to be that boring."

Mark looked over at him. He smiled. "What are you thinking?"

Eddie smiled too. It was like watching a couple of vultures smiling at each other over the body of a cow.

"Oh…" He shrugged modestly. "I was just thinking that space isn't the only place where no one can hear you scream." He laughed unpleasantly. "We might be able to amuse ourselves a bit, you know."

Mark has always been the perfect sidekick. When Eddie sang the Womble song to me all those years ago, it was Mark who joined in the chorus.

"How?" Mark was looking at Eddie with admiration and real interest.

Eddie's smile grew more intense. It was enough to give me the creeps.

"I think our good friend Archie Spongo might be able to help us with that."

Mark cackled. *"Our good friend Archie Spongo..."* He scooped up a fistful of crisps and chomped them into mush. *"Our good friend Archie Spongo... That's funny."*

"And it could be true," said Eddie.

Mark stopped chomping. "What?"

Eddie picked up a single crisp and stared at it in a thoughtful way. "Why not? Archie doesn't have any other friends, does he? He's going to be all alone. Unless we declare a truce..."

"Declare a truce?"

"Mark Crother, the human echo," muttered Kuba.

Eddie nodded. "That's right, you heard it here first. We declare a truce, and make friends with the boy from planet Weirdo."

Mark frowned thoughtfully. "But we're not friends with him," he said. And then, in case Eddie had overlooked this important fact, he added, "He's a geek."

Eddie sighed. "Yeah, I know he's a geek, Mark. But Archie doesn't know he's a geek, does he? If we say we want to hang out with him on the trip he's not going to wonder why. He'll jump at the chance."

Mark was looking at Eddie the way Watson looked at Sherlock Holmes when he worked out that a one-legged man smoking a cigar from Eastern Europe had committed the crime.

"You mean get him to think we want to be friends and then really have some fun?"

"Exactly," said Eddie. "Think of it: alone in our room … up in the mountains…"

I shook my head as the image began to fade. "Eddie's wasted in secondary school," I said. "He should be a politician."

"He probably will be," said Kuba. The blue monsters reappeared, but Kuba didn't go back to her game. She pushed back the chair, nearly running over my toes. "The question is, what are you going to do about it? It's one thing abandoning *me*, your best friend, but you can't stay at home and leave Archie unprotected for five whole days."

"You protect him," I said. "You're the one on a mission from heaven."

Kuba got that stubborn look on her face. "I can't interfere, and you know it." She sounded so sincere that anyone who didn't know her better than I did would have believed her.

Not interfering is Rule Number One if you happen to be an angel. Angels can guide and direct, but they're not supposed to actually meddle. This is a rule I've never seen Kuba pay much attention to.

"Just a minute." I held my hand up like a policeman stopping traffic. "You interfered when it came to stopping the bulldozers."

My mother, her environmental group, Keep Our Planet Green, and Mr Bamber all held me totally responsible for stopping the bulldozers, but the truth is that I had some help. At a crucial point in my negotiations with the security guards, Kuba Bamber raised the dead. It wasn't the sight of me sitting in the mud holding a SAVE OUR WOODS sign that made the bulldozers turn round – it was the sight of several hundred restless ghosts moving towards them.

"Don't think it wasn't noticed," said Kuba. "I have very strict instructions now."

"And so do I. My grandmother says I should stay in bed and drink plenty of liquids."

"Mrs Bamber will give you a lift to the bus," said Kuba. "Save your mother having to drive you in the milk float."

"You're wasting your breath," I told her. "I'm not going. Elmo has spoken."

"We'll be leaving the house at quarter to eight," Kuba continued. "Make sure you're ready."

I opened my mouth to repeat the bit about wasting her breath, but I didn't say it because for the first time I noticed Kuba's feet. They were the same feet she's always had, but they were wearing something new – state-of-the-art Reebok trainers with reflective trim and a plastic wedge in the heel that glowed in the dark. They were the most incredibly beautiful shoes I'd ever seen.

"Where'd you get those?" I was practically whispering with awe.

"Mrs Bamber bought them for me," said Kuba. "I like my old trainers better."

"You're mad." I couldn't take my eyes off her shoes. No one in the whole school had a pair that came close to them. *I'd give anything to have a pair of trainers like those,* I thought.

And that's when Kuba started shaking my hand.

"Elmo Blue," cried Kuba. "You've got yourself a deal. They're yours. I'll bring them over in the morning. You can wear them on the trip."

I stopped looking at her feet and looked at her instead.

"Hang on," I protested. "I didn't mean—"

"A deal's a deal," said Kuba.

"But my mother won't let me keep them," I argued. "You know how she feels about Reebok."

Kuba squeezed my hand. "Oh, she'll let you

36

keep them," she assured me. "Don't you worry about a thing."

My eyes went back to the trainers. They really were phenomenal.

"OK," I relented. "I'll go. For the shoes. But I'm not protecting anybody but myself, is that clear? I am not getting involved in Archie Spongo's problems."

"Pack a torch," said Kuba. "You never know when it might come in handy."

BOMB VOYAGE

Kuba brought the trainers over the next morning. She told my mother they were a present from her and Mrs Bamber to thank me for saving the woods. My mother thought this was such a lovely gesture that she didn't even hear the word "Reebok".

The trainers looked even more brilliant in daylight. I put them on straight away. Since Kuba's much taller than I am, I was afraid they'd be too big, but somehow they fitted me perfectly.

"They look cool," said Kuba.

"They look very nice," said my mother.

Gertie liked the way they glowed in the dark.

At exactly seven forty-five, as Kuba had promised, we pulled out of the Bambers' drive in Mrs Bamber's silver Porsche. I sat in the back, admiring my feet the entire way.

Things didn't start to go wrong until we actually got on the bus.

There were four teachers on the trip: Mr Palfry, Mrs Smiley, Ms Kaye and Mr Bombay. Three of them were already on the bus by the time we arrived, but Mr Palfry was standing by the door with a clipboard, checking everybody off as they climbed the steps. Despite these precautions, there was a mad scramble to get on and get the best seats.

Kuba was ahead of me. I caught a glimpse of Eddie and Mark at the back of the bus as we shuffled up the aisle. I tugged at Kuba's arm. "Let's sit up here," I suggested.

Kuba was looking straight ahead of her. "Where angels fear to tread..." she said softly.

I wasn't sure what she meant. In my experience of angels, they don't fear to tread anywhere. I peered round her arm. Archie Spongo was sitting in the seat in front of Mark and Eddie, smiling in his bewildered, hopeful way.

The idea that, just perhaps, we should have warned Archie about Eddie's master plan sort of whizzed through my mind.

Kuba turned round to look at me. "It's too late for that," she said, as though I'd spoken out loud. "You'll have to go to plan B."

Since I hadn't realized that there was a plan A, I had no idea what plan B was meant to be.

"What?" I asked.

But Kuba wasn't looking at me any more. Someone was calling her.

"Kuba! Kuba!" It was Ariel Moordock. Ariel was right at the front by the door. She was patting the seat beside her in an enthusiastic way. "Come and sit with me!" she called.

Personally, I couldn't work out why Kuba liked Ariel. She reminded me of a Barbie doll because of her blonde ponytail and the fact that she always wore pink. And she never stopped talking – a Barbie doll wired for sound.

"You, of all people, shouldn't judge a book by its cover," Kuba hissed in my ear. And then she smiled back at Ariel. "Brilliant!" she shouted.

I gaped at her with a look that I could only hope expressed the total horror I was feeling.

Hey, what about me? I was thinking. *Who am I meant to sit with?*

Kuba smiled. "The correct word is *whom*, not *who*," she said helpfully.

I was really irked. I hate it when she corrects my English, and I hate it when she reads my mind, but at that moment what I really hated was the fact that I knew exactly what *she* was thinking.

"No," I whispered. I shook my head. "I don't care what you say. I'm not sitting with Archie Spongo."

Kuba, however, wasn't there. While I was

shaking my head and being firm, she somehow got past me and slipped into the seat beside Ariel.

"Elmo!" It was Mr Palfry. He was standing by the door, waving his clipboard in my direction. "Elmo, you're blocking the way. Go and sit next to Archie. I want to get this show on the road."

We hadn't even left the car park and already I didn't like the way things were going. Being forced to sit next to Archie was a complication I hadn't counted on, but I thought of Bill Gates, living on junk food and working for nothing all those years, and I took courage. *Never say die*, I told myself. *It's always darkest before the dawn... You can lead a horse to water but you can't make it drink...*

Sitting with Archie didn't have to change my position. I had my trainers; all I had to do was survive the next few days and I'd be able to enjoy them. I might have to sit next to Archie, but I didn't have to look after him. I didn't even have to talk to him if I didn't want to.

I squeezed past him to the window seat, and then I folded my arms across my stomach and stared straight ahead, preparing myself for a long, silent journey.

Eddie and Mark were too busy mucking about at first to pay much attention to either Archie or me. You'd think they'd escaped from their cage, the way they carried on. They talked and joked behind us; they kicked our seats and threw crisps at each other; they fought over whose turn it was on Eddie's Game Boy.

Every once in a while one of them would remember they were meant to be friends with Archie and would call out, "Right, Archie?" as though he had some vague idea of what they were talking about.

Archie always nodded and said, "Right."

And every once in a while one of them would lean over the seat and point something out through the window – "Look, Archie, there's a horse!" or "Look, Archie, there's a water tower!" – and Archie would look and nod as though he'd never seen a horse or a water tower before.

I decided on a policy of invisibility. I pretended I wasn't there. So even though I really love chess, I said I didn't want to play a game of chess on Archie's travel set. I also didn't want to play a game of draughts. And I also didn't want to hear about Archie's dog.

"It's not really mine; it's my aunt's," explained Archie. "It can say 'I love you', 'hello' and 'sausages'."

Laughter spluttered behind us.

"Sau-sa-ges," said Eddie in a deep, thick voice. "Sau-sa-ges."

"I don't really like dogs," I lied.

Archie said, "Oh."

He wanted to know if I'd like half of his chocolate bar.

I said I didn't care for chocolate either.

Mark said, "Yeah, thanks!" – and snatched the whole bar out of his hand.

Archie smiled. Then he reached in his pocket and took out another packet. "Gum?" asked Archie.

Eddie took the gum.

I slumped down in my seat and stared out of the window, being invisible and uninvolved.

Archie finally gave up trying to talk to me. He got out a book and started to read. I became absorbed in watching the traffic and the occasional sheep or cow. The movement of the coach made me sleepy and relaxed. I was drifting off, thinking about my new trainers, when Archie put his book away and took something else out of his bag.

I glanced over. He was holding a metal box on his lap. I'd never seen anything like it before. As my grandmother always says, "Curiosity killed the cat", and curiosity made me reckless.

"What's that?" I asked.

"I've got my lunch in it." I was used to seeing Archie smile, but this smile was different. He was really pleased. "Isn't it great? My dad gave it to me. It's his mess kit from the army."

Which explained why I didn't recognize it; the Blues are not a military family.

"Yeah," I said. "It's cool."

This was all the encouragement Archie needed. He held up the mess kit so I could get a better look.

Which meant that Mark and Eddie got a better look too, of course.

"Hey, what's that?" Eddie whistled sharply. "I don't believe it! Archie's got a bomb!"

There was a splutter of mirth behind us, and then Mark joined in.

"Archie's got a bomb!" he echoed.

"Watch out!" hollered Eddie. "Spongo's armed!"

People looked up from their lunches and conversations, curious as cats.

The usual smile of confusion settled on Archie's face. He laughed nervously. He knew there was a joke, but, as often happened, he wasn't sure what it was.

Then Jamie Keegan, who was sitting behind Mark and Eddie, started to chant. "Bomb ... bomb ... bomb ... bomb..." boomed Jamie. "Bomb ... bomb ... bomb ... bomb..."

More kids looked up.

Mark hurled himself on the floor, his arms over his head. "It's going to go off!" he screamed. "It's going to go off!"

Archie laughed when everyone else laughed. I don't know how she knew what was going on, since as far as I could tell she hadn't stopped talking since Kuba sat down, but Ariel Moordock started to scream. She sounded like a really fast dentist's drill.

Mrs Smiley shot up from her seat like a jack-in-the-box.

"Quiet!" she shouted. "Everybody quiet! For heaven's sake, Ariel, stop shrieking like that."

Not only did Ariel not stop shrieking like that, but the rest of the girls started shrieking like that too. Except, that was, for Kuba Bamber. Kuba turned round and looked at me. She was glaring.

I slumped down a bit more in my seat and looked away.

"Bomb! Bomb! Bomb!" shrieked Ariel. "Archie's got a bomb!"

"Don't be ridiculous!" roared Mrs Smiley. "Archie's got his lunch."

Staggering a bit as the bus veered round a bend, Mr Palfry stepped into the aisle.

"Calm down!" He clapped his hands. "Everybody just calm down! Now!"

"Bomb ... bomb ... bomb," grunted the boys. "Bomb ... bomb ... bomb..."

Archie continued to sit there with that stupid smile on his face. I felt like shaking him. I felt like screaming at him to stop smiling. *Stop smiling!* I wanted to shout. *Can't you see you have nothing to smile about?*

"Pull over!" Mr Palfry bawled at the driver. "Pull over at once!"

The driver glanced at him in the rear-view mirror. "This is a luxury coach, sir, not a Mini," the driver informed him. "I can't just stop because you tell me to."

It was while Mrs Smiley was trying to calm everybody down and Mr Palfry was yelling at the driver that Eddie made his move. He reached over the seat and grabbed the mess kit from Archie's hands.

Archie was like a rabbit frozen in the head-lights of a car; he didn't even try to get it back. He just sat there, looking at his empty hands as if he couldn't work out what had happened.

Eddie tossed the mess kit to Mark.

"Bomb!" shouted Mark, holding it over his head. "Watch out for the bomb!"

That broke the spell. Archie started shaking like my grandfather's vibrating chair. "My dad's mess kit!" he wailed. "My dad's mess kit!"

"Eddie!" Mr Palfry was looking a bit red in the face from shouting loud enough to be heard. "Eddie, give me that this instant!"

Eddie held up his empty hands. "I haven't got it, sir."

"My dad's mess kit!" wailed Archie. "My dad's mess kit!"

If I hadn't been following a policy of non-involvement, I would have told him to shut up, that he was only making it worse. But I was invisible, so I didn't.

"Mark Crother!" roared Mr Palfry. "Either you give me that box right now or we're turning round and going home."

Mark looked really surprised to discover that Mr Palfry was so upset.

"We're only mucking around, sir." He held the kit up. "Here! Catch!"

Mr Spongo's mess kit flew through the air in a pretty bomb-like way.

To give him credit, Mr Palfry almost caught it, but he was sort of pinned in the aisle and didn't have much mobility. His fingers stretched, but all they touched was air. The mess kit sailed past them, heading for disaster, otherwise known as the windscreen of our luxury coach.

It was Kuba Bamber who stopped it. Except for the driver, who was trying to drive, she was the only person not watching the progress of Mr Spongo's mess kit. She was standing up to get her own lunch box from the rack. If she had been any shorter, it would have gone right over her head. And if she hadn't been wearing her old wide-brimmed hat, it probably would have knocked her out.

"Kuba!" cried Mr Palfry. "Are you all right?"

Calm amid the general hysteria, Kuba picked up the mess kit and handed it to Mr Palfry.

"I'm fine," she assured him. Her sweet smile turned to a look of concern. "But I'm afraid the box is dented."

The bus wheezed to the side of the road.

Looking shaken, Mr Palfry leaned against his seat. "All right now, just settle down!" He put on his most intimidating face and turned to Eddie and Mark. "I'll talk to you two later." He took the mess kit from Kuba and gave it back to its rightful owner. "Are you all right, Archie?" asked Mr Palfry.

Archie burst into tears.

WELCOME TO WYNDACH

After he calmed Archie down, Mr Palfry had his talk with Mark and Eddie. He was cold and angry, and Mark and Eddie were apologetic and desperate not to be misunderstood.

I closed my eyes, so Mr Palfry would know I wasn't involved.

"We're really really sorry, Mr Palfry," said Eddie. His voice was limp with sincerity. "Really sorry. We were just having some fun, weren't we, Mark? We didn't mean any harm."

"Yeah," agreed Mark. "We were just having some fun."

Eddie put a hand on Archie's shoulder. "We never meant to get you so upset, Archie," said Eddie. "You're our friend."

It was enough to break your heart.

Archie swallowed hard. "I know we're friends," he mumbled. "I know you were having fun. It's just that it was my dad's mess kit…" He cleared his throat. "Perhaps I reacted too much."

"You did," said Eddie. "You reacted much too much. You took it all wrong. It was just a joke."

I opened my eyes. I was almost tempted to interrupt this heart-wrenching scene with some pointed remark of my own (something like, *Yeah, a joke like World War II was a joke*), but I managed to resist.

"You know, just a joke between mates," Eddie went on. "We're really sorry, Archie," he repeated. "We won't do anything like that again."

I nearly laughed out loud at that. *Yeah, sure,* I thought. *Not until the next time.*

Mr Palfry, however, didn't share my cynicism.

"Well, I should hope not," said Mr Palfry. "I expect this to be the end of it."

"Say you forgive us," pleaded Eddie. His hand jutted out between me and Archie. "Say we're still friends."

Archie reached up and shook Eddie's hand. "Friends," agreed Archie.

I closed my eyes again.

Camp Wyndach was as like Disneyland Paris as a milk float is like a silver Porsche. There were no bright lights, no rides, no Mickey Mouse, no nothing except for vegetation. My mother would have loved it. It was stuck in the middle of what Mr Palfry described as a picturesque valley.

"This is a very picturesque valley," said Mr Palfry grandly. He gestured towards the trees, and the mountains, and the mud. "It's a favourite spot for photographers and painters."

It was unfortunate that there weren't any painters or photographers on the bus with us. Despite Mr Palfry's enthusiasm nobody else looked particularly excited as we churned down the narrow, muddy trail.

Ariel pointed through the windscreen. "Is that *it*?" she asked. She sounded as if she'd been hoping for a little more.

Way down at the end of the rut we were in, you could see a few rustic hovels huddled in the shadows of the mountains. From where we were, they looked like they were probably left over from some prehistoric settlement.

Mr Palfry nodded happily. "That's it! Isn't it terrific?"

No one – not even one of the other teachers – actually answered this question one way or the other. Ariel wasn't the only one who'd been hoping for a little more.

As we got closer you could see that the rustic hovels were several small wooden cabins and two larger stone lodges.

In her pink tracksuit and pink anorak, Ariel looked like a Barbie doll that's just suffered a major disappointment. "Does it have indoor toilets?" she asked.

"Of course it does," Mr Palfry assured her. He laughed. "*And* electricity."

"Well, thank God for that," said Ariel.

Personally, at that exact moment I wouldn't have cared if we had to dig our own trenches and rub two sticks together to get a fire going. I had other things on my mind. The calm after the bomb scare had started me brooding and the horrible truth had finally dawned on me. Despite what I'd told her about me and Eddie, and despite what I thought we'd agreed, Kuba Bamber had set me up. She'd never intended to sit with me on the bus. She'd probably had a pretty good idea all along of what might happen between Archie and Eddie, and she'd expected me to intervene. *Me!* It was the sort of devious thing angels do. The fact that I'd managed to stay invisible despite her interference made me feel almost proud, but I could see that I was going to have to make a very firm stand – to state my position clearly – before she did something else to get me involved.

I was one of the first off the bus. I wanted a quiet word with Mr and Mrs Bamber's adopted daughter before she disappeared into the girls' lodge and I lost any chance of talking to her alone.

You'd think Kuba knew I was waiting for

her, the amount of time it took her to get off the bus. Everyone else gathered round the luggage hold while she made a big production of checking under the seat and up in the rack to make sure neither she nor Ariel had left anything behind.

"Oh, I don't know…" Kuba was saying as she and Ariel finally came slowly down the steps. "I think it's really interesting here. Try to picture it when it was a Roman outpost."

"It still looks like a Roman outpost," said Ariel. "And anyway, what's the big deal? The whole of Britain was a Roman outpost."

I grabbed Kuba's arm.

"I want to talk to you," I said. I smiled.

"Not now," said Kuba. "We can talk at supper."

But I wasn't going to be fooled by the old "we can talk at supper" ploy.

"No," I said firmly. "Now." I yanked her round to the comparative privacy of the front of the bus.

Kuba straightened her hat. "What's the matter with you, Elmo? I don't want to be the last to get my bag."

"Never mind your bag. You and I have something to discuss."

"Oh, really?" I could tell she was acting because she looked so totally blameless and surprised. "And what's that?"

I told her what it was.

"What's the big idea?" I demanded. "First you beg me to come so you won't be on your own, and then you stick me with Archie Spongo."

"I didn't stick you with anyone," said Kuba, calm as a stone. "Mr Palfry's the one who told you to sit with him."

But I knew her too well to be fooled by that.

"Hah!" I said. "Mr Palfry had nothing to do with it, and you know it."

"Elmo," said Kuba, sounding like the most reasonable person on the planet, "they're getting the bags out – Ariel's waiting."

I was still holding her arm. I tightened my grip.

"I am not here to protect Archie Spongo," I told her. "I do not want to be involved in his problems. I do not want to be involved with Eddie and Mark. I want to stay as far away from the lot of them as I can get."

"You're a free agent," said Kuba. "You can do what you want."

"I want you to promise that you'll stop interfering," I said. "As of now."

Kuba gazed at me with the innocence of a violet.

"Me? You know I don't interfere, Elmo." She smiled shyly. "It's not allowed."

"Just promise that you won't," I insisted. "I don't want any trouble."

"So don't have any." Kuba turned to go, but I held tight.

"Promise. Say the words. Say, 'Elmo, I promise you I won't interfere in your life any more.'"

Kuba sighed heavily. "Elmo," she said in a sing-song voice, "I promise you I won't interfere in your life any more."

As promises go, it lacked warmth and spontaneity, but it covered the main points.

I let go of her arm. "Good. I just want to have a peaceful, boring time like everyone else."

"Boring?" Kuba's smile was amused. She gestured to the old huts and the dark old woods, not a neon sign or souvenir shop in sight. "How could you have a boring time *here*?"

"I don't know," I said, "but I'm looking forward to finding out."

As luck would have it, my bag was the last one to come out of the hold.

I watched the driver's feet wave up and down as he lay on his stomach and shone his torch into the darkness.

"There it is!" he cried. "Right in the corner." He gave it a tug. "I don't know how it got back there," he grunted as he pulled it towards the opening. "Those rough roads must have shifted it."

Everyone else was already inside by the time I got to the lodge. They were all sitting on the floor. Mrs Smiley was sitting on a bench that looked like a log, giving everyone the usual lecture about working together and co-operating and not giving the teachers or each other a hard time. Then she started going through the details of daily life in the wilderness. Everybody looked pretty bored.

Kuba and Ariel were up at the front, so I slipped in at the back next to Carl and Jamal.

Mrs Smiley said that the two lodges would be known as A and B, and that the girls would sleep in A, the one we were in, and the boys would sleep in B.

"There are four beds in each room, and each lodge has two loos," said Mrs Smiley. She clapped her hands together. "Since we have a few people absent with the flu, it works out perfectly."

Ariel raised her hand. "Are there showers or baths?" she wanted to know.

"Metal tubs and a big kettle," called Eddie.

Mr Palfry said, "Shhh!"

Mrs Smiley laughed good-naturedly. "Showers," she informed Ariel. And she told us where they were, and where the kitchen was, and where the dining room was.

Then they split us up and Mr Palfry started giving out the boys' rooms while Mrs Smiley gave out the ones for the girls.

Things went smoothly until he got to Mark

and Eddie. Mark and Eddie wanted to share with Archie and Jamie.

Mr Palfry shook his head. "No, Eddie," he said. He put on his stern, no-nonsense face. "Not Jamie. Jamie just eggs you and Mark on. You'll have to find someone else." His eyes ran round the room. "Does anyone want to bunk with Eddie, Archie and Mark?"

The boys who didn't have a room yet all looked at the floor. There were knots in the wooden boards that made it look as if it was smiling back at me.

"Come on, you lot," urged Mr Palfry. "Who's going to volunteer?"

If you asked me, it would be like volunteering to walk into a nest of vipers.

Mr Palfry tapped his pen on his clipboard. "Let's remember what Mrs Smiley said about team spirit and working together," urged Mr Palfry. "Who wants to swap with Jamie?"

The face in the floorboards agreed with me; it looked as if it winked.

"Elmo!" Mr Palfry was the happiest he'd sounded since the bomb scare. "Brilliant. At least someone understands about teamwork."

I looked up, my mouth open. "But—"

Mr Palfry's eyes were on his clipboard. "That'll be Elmo, Archie, Eddie and Mark in room 3B."

"But Mr Palfry!" I shouted. "Mr Palfry, I didn't volunteer."

57

Mr Palfry's happiness vanished as quickly as it had come. "Of course you did," he snapped. "You put your hand up."

This was wrong. This could not be. In my worst fantasy about the class trip, I'd never considered this possibility for a second – not even for less than a second.

"But Mr Palfry—"

Mr Palfry's attention had returned to his clipboard. "So that means Carl, Jamal, Andy and Jamie are in 6B."

"Can you believe it?" said a voice a lot sweeter than honey behind me. "Ariel and I are in 3A."

I looked round. Kuba and Ariel were passing by with their bags, headed, I assumed, for room 3A.

Kuba's smile was so sweet I felt as if I was stuck to it.

"It's quite a coincidence, isn't it?" said Kuba.

"Yeah," I said, my heart sinking somewhere round my toes. "It certainly is."

NIGHT ONE AND COUNTING

"When my sister was at Campton they went skiing," Ariel was saying. She had some fluffy pink things in her hair that bounced every time she moved her head. They were pretty hypnotic. "They stayed in a chalet and there was a disco in the main hotel every night and a whole room of arcade games. Now that's my idea of a cool school trip." She waved her hand at the picturesque scene of rampant vegetation beyond the dining room window. "This is my idea of hell."

Kuba smiled over her bread and butter. "It's nothing like hell," said Kuba. "Hell's much more like Harrods on the first day of the January sales."

I'd never been to Harrods (my mother has principles about that too, of course), but I laughed. I was feeling better now that I was finally away from my room-mates. It turned my stomach to see Mark and Eddie making up to Archie. I'd unpacked as quickly and invisibly as I could, but I'd still found it pretty stressful. Eddie and Mark were neither quick nor invisible. They kept up a constant stream of jokes while they unpacked, amusing themselves by going through Archie's things and teasing him about everything from his pyjamas to his toothbrush. Any time Archie looked a little more bewildered than usual, they'd whack him on the back and say, "All right, Archie? All right, mate?" And Archie would laugh and nod and say everything was all right. It was like watching a lamb being petted as it was taken to the slaughterhouse.

"I'm surprised you volunteered to share with Mark and Eddie," said Ariel. "I didn't think you three were friends."

"We're not," I said. "I didn't exactly volunteer." I flicked a meaningful look at Kuba out of the corners of my eyes. "There was a bit of a mix-up."

Ignoring my meaningfulness, Kuba turned to me with another of her impossibly sweet and gentle smiles. "What mix-up was that?" I could practically hear harps playing in the background. "Mr Palfry saw you put up your hand."

"Mr Palfry saw *someone* put up *a* hand," I corrected her. "That doesn't mean it was me, or mine."

Kuba, of course, didn't blink. "You were at the back of the room," she reminded me. "If it wasn't yours, it must have been the hand of God."

Only Ariel thought this was a joke.

"Poor you," said Ariel. I hadn't noticed it before, but she had a very sympathetic smile. "Eddie and Mark are *sooo* juvenile."

Juvenile wasn't quite the word I'd choose to describe Eddie and Mark – psychopathic seemed more accurate – but it was close enough. I started to revise my opinion of Ariel. She still reminded me of a Barbie doll, but she was obviously much more intelligent.

"It's Archie I feel sorry for," said my loyal friend, Kuba Bamber. "They never stop taking the mickey out of him, and he has no idea how to fight back."

"Heavy artillery might help," said Ariel.

I decided to stay non-committal. "Boys will be boys..." I muttered vaguely.

Kuba humphed. "You wouldn't say that if it was you they were picking on, Elmo Blue." She looked at her fork in a critical way. "If you ask me, it's about time somebody stood up to those two."

"That'll be the day," said Ariel. "Amy Johnson told them off once for nicking her glitter nail polish and painting Mrs Smiley's desk with it, and they put her telephone number up in the phone box outside the pub. Mr Johnson

61

nearly had a fit." Ariel brushed some crumbs from her fluffy pink jumper. "Anyway, it *was* pretty funny about the bomb, wasn't it? You have to admit that." She glanced over to the liveliest table in the dining room. "And they do seem to be getting on all right now."

I reckoned it depended on what you meant by "getting on all right". Mark and Eddie, on opposite sides of the table, were flicking tiny bread missiles at each other. Everybody seemed to think this was hilarious, even Archie Spongo, who happened to be sitting right in the line of fire. There were crumbs all over his plate, but he kept smiling and laughing with the others.

"That's what they said when they were building the Tower of Babel," said Kuba. "It's getting on all right now..." She scooped up some peas with her fork. "That was just before it fell apart."

I didn't know much about the Tower of Babel, but things started falling apart in room 3B almost as soon as the door shut behind us for the night.

Archie couldn't find his pyjamas. "They cannot walk," he kept saying over and over. "Where can they be?"

He took everything out of his drawer and put it all back.

"They're not there," he said. He was looking at me, but he was talking to his good friends Eddie and Mark.

Eddie climbed up to his bunk. "Search me," he said. He gave Archie a friendly, matey grin. "What would I want with your pyjamas?"

Archie blinked. "Well…" He obviously thought this was a reasonable question.

Mark snuggled under his covers. "Don't look at me." He sounded as if he was already half asleep. "I like the pyjamas I have."

Archie stared at his open drawer as though there was some possibility that in the last few minutes his pyjamas had decided to return. "But what will I do?"

Eddie yawned again. "You'll just have to sleep in your underwear, won't you?" he mumbled.

Unfortunately Archie couldn't sleep in his underwear, not unless he wanted to die of hypothermia. His pyjamas weren't all that had disappeared – his blankets had gone too.

"I'd lend you one of mine," said Eddie, "but I'm very sensitive to the cold."

"Me too," said Mark. "See!" He stuck his foot out from under his warm blankets. "I even sleep in my socks."

Archie looked at me again. Mark and Eddie looked at me too. Archie's look said, *Help me!* but the look Eddie and Mark were giving me said, *Don't you dare!*

They didn't have to worry. I, for one, had

no intention of daring anything. So far my policy of being invisible was working just fine.

"I haven't been feeling that well," I told Archie. It was more or less the truth. "I've got to keep warm." I rolled over to end the discussion.

"Do you think someone took them for a joke?" asked Archie.

"Probably," said Eddie. "You know what this lot's like."

"Yeah," said Mark. "Probably someone took them for a joke."

"I'm going to tell Mr Palfry," Archie decided.

"I wouldn't do that," said Eddie. "Mr Palfry's been in a bad mood all day. You'll just make him angry."

"Yeah," agreed Mark. "I wouldn't do that."

"But why should he be angry with *me*?" asked Archie reasonably. "*I* haven't done anything wrong."

Archie went off to get Mr Palfry.

As soon as the door shut, Eddie and Mark were out of their beds. They weren't tired any more. They raced about, putting Archie's pyjamas and blankets back where they'd found them.

"You'll keep your mouth shut, Elmo, if you know what's good for you," Eddie warned the back of my head.

I was pretty sure I knew what was good for me. I started to snore.

Mr Palfry marched into the room like a guard in a film who's been dragged from his dinner to sort out one of the prisoners.

"What'd I tell you lot?" he demanded. "It's been a long day. I'm in no mood for your games."

"Games?" Eddie's voice was hazy with exhaustion. "We haven't done anything, sir. I swear. I was practically asleep."

Also practically asleep, I rolled over so I could see what was going on.

Mr Palfry looked from Eddie to Archie's bunk. Then he looked at Archie.

"And what do you call those?" asked Mr Palfry.

Eager to demonstrate his improving grasp of English, Archie answered immediately. "Blankets," he said, and then stopped in confusion. He blinked. "But, sir—"

Mr Palfry was holding on to his patience the way a bat hangs on to the roof of a cave. "Let's have a look for those pyjamas, shall we?" he asked in a really tight voice.

"They're not in my drawer, sir," Archie insisted. "I told you, I removed everything."

Mr Palfry, however, was already opening Archie's drawer. Carefully and methodically, like the man of science he is, he too removed everything from the drawer. The pyjamas were at the bottom. He lifted them out and handed them to Archie.

"Perhaps you forgot where you put them," suggested Mr Palfry. "We all forget things when we're tired."

Archie opened his mouth, but he didn't say anything.

"I know this is your first school trip, Archie," Mr Palfry went on, "so you're probably nervous as well as tired." He gave Archie a smile that was meant to be sympathetic, but I thought looked a bit threatening. "What do you say we just forget about this little incident? All right?"

"It's all right with us," said Eddie generously. "We just want to get some sleep. We've got a big day tomorrow, haven't we?"

"Yes," said Mr Palfry. "We most certainly have."

It took me about two seconds to fall asleep. Partly because I was exhausted from the stresses and traumas of the day, and partly because if anything more was going to happen that night I really wanted to miss it.

I had a dream.

In my dream I was on the school trip. I was wearing my new trainers, and everybody thought they were really cool. Eddie and Mark were desperate to sit with me. For some reason I was pretty chuffed about that. I thought it meant they liked me. In real life I didn't care if they liked me or not as long as they didn't torment me, but in my dream it was tremendously important that they did. Neither Kuba nor Archie was in my dream. The camp was different too. Instead of the rustic cabins and lodges of Camp Wyndach, we were staying in a modern hotel with bright lights and an indoor pool. Eddie, Mark and I all shared a room. Mr Palfry stuck his head round the door and said goodnight, and then he turned out the lights and I fell asleep.

The weird thing was that even though I was asleep, I was sort of awake at the same time. I could hear the others whispering and moving around, but for some reason I didn't think anything of it. They lifted up my bed and carried it out of the room. I knew what they were doing, but I didn't seem to care. It wasn't until I heard the laughter that I woke up.

In my dream I opened my eyes. My bed was in the lobby of the hotel. Everybody was standing around it – not just everyone from my class and the teachers, but other guests at the hotel and bellboys and people like that. Even the bus driver was there. But it wasn't all the laughing people who caught my attention. It was my feet. Instead of my new, to-die-for trainers, my feet were wearing my old Womble slippers. The really bizarre thing is that for a second I was really happy to see the slippers.

I woke up when the people in my dream all started singing, "Remember you're a Womble."

I lay there for a few seconds, just catching my breath. I was damp with sweat and my heart was pounding. *What a nightmare,* I thought. *It was worse than the dream where you turn up for school in your pyjamas.*

The word "pyjamas" repeated itself in my head. *Pyjamas … pyjamas … everyone seeing you in your pyjamas.*

Kuba's words sort of drifted through my head as well. *You wouldn't say that if it was you they were picking on … if it was you … you … if it was you…*

And that's when I realized what was really happening. It wasn't me being humiliated in front of everyone – it was Archie.

I looked over just in time to see Mark and Eddie carrying him through the door. He was sound asleep in his striped pyjamas.

There are times in life when you simply don't know what the right thing to do is. And then there are other times in life when you do know what the right thing to do is, but you also know that you're not going to do it.

The door clicked shut and I sighed. I knew what the right thing to do would be. The right thing to do would be to charge after them like the Lone Ranger and stop Mark and Eddie immediately. But I also knew that I definitely wasn't going to do the right thing. It would have been all right for someone like the Lone Ranger – the Lone Ranger wouldn't have to share a room with Eddie and Mark for the next five days. The Lone Ranger would stop them and then gallop off in a cloud of dust to sort out someone else. No, I wasn't going to come close to doing the right thing; stopping them was getting involved with a capital I.

I pushed back the covers and sat up. As long as I was awake, I reckoned I might as well go to the toilet. That wasn't getting involved; that was a call of nature.

Kuba Bamber's voice was still floating through my mind as I pulled on my trainers. *What if it was you…? What if it was you…?*

It wasn't me, though, I kept telling myself; it was someone else. I opened the door and tip-toed into the silent dark.

The toilet was in the middle of the first-floor hallway. There was no light showing through the crack. I put my ear to the door. They weren't in there.

What if it was you…? Kuba's voice kept yammering in my head. *What if it was you … was you…?*

I decided that the toilet could wait. I wanted to see where Eddie and Mark had gone with Archie.

I suppose I thought they'd leave him in the main room where the whole lodge would be sure to see him in the morning, but as I got to the top of the stairs I heard the front door shut very softly.

They can't leave him outside, I told myself. *The cold will wake him up.*

Barely breathing, I crept down the stairs and slid through the front door. I crouched down on the porch behind the railing. The night was dark and cool and full of strange sounds. My blood tingled and my nerves were sharp. I didn't feel like me. I felt like someone much braver and wilder. Someone who wasn't afraid of anything.

I could just make out Mark and Eddie, Archie swinging gently between them. Archie might have trouble with the English language and the English sense of humour, but he had no trouble sleeping, I'll say that for him. They were heading for the girls' lodge.

You almost had to admire Eddie and Mark. Leaving Archie where Mr Palfry, Mr Bombay and the rest of the boys would find him was bad enough; but leaving him where Mrs Smiley, Ms Kaye and all the girls would find him was diabolically clever.

I pictured myself in my Womble slippers, waking up in the girls' lodge. It was enough to make you wish you'd been born a frog instead of a person. And that's when I realized that I was probably going to do something after all. Not much, perhaps, but something. I'd see where Eddie and Mark left Archie, and then as soon as they'd gone I'd wake him up. Anonymously, like the Lone Ranger. *Who woke me up?* Archie would wonder groggily. *Who was that masked man?* If Mark or Eddie got back to the room before I did, I'd tell them the truth, that I'd gone to the toilet.

A shadow darkened the entrance to the opposite lodge. Still feeling like someone more confident and brave, I crept down the steps.

There was nothing between the two lodges but the open space of the car park. I took another deep breath and, staying as low to the ground as I could, I hurled myself forward.

I was halfway to the girls' lodge when I heard the scream. The hair stood up on the back of my neck, just like people say it does when you're terrified out of your mind. I threw myself flat on the ground and froze as though I'd been zapped by lightning.

I recognized that scream. It was Ariel Moordock. I couldn't see her face, but I could see a figure in one of the bedroom windows on the first floor. I willed her to go back to bed.

Ariel paid no attention to my thought waves. She screamed again, and then she started shouting as if she was in a disaster film. Because there isn't any traffic or anything like that in the middle of nowhere, every bat, owl and wildcat in the area could hear her loud and clear.

"Mrs Smiley! Mrs Smiley!" Ariel was shouting. "Mrs Smiley! Come quick! There's a ghost

71

in the car park!"

Not only could the wildlife hear her, every human in the area heard her too. Lights went on in both the lodges.

I didn't know what to do. I could hear footsteps thundering down the stairs of the boys' lodge. I reckoned it was Mr Palfry. If I didn't get out of the way, he'd probably trip over me as he charged to the rescue. *What would a soldier do in this situation?* I asked myself. My mother severely monitors my video viewing, but I'd seen enough war films to be able to answer my question. A soldier would crawl backwards until he got to the safety of the shrubs that bordered the boys' lodge. I started crawling backwards. I reckoned soldiers must have special training in this sort of thing, because crawling backwards wasn't as easy as it looked in films. The ground was soft and uneven, and my knees kept getting in the way.

I was still several metres from the safety of the shrubs when the porch light went on behind me and the door to the boys' lodge was flung open.

I stopped breathing and closed my eyes, waiting for Mr Palfry to start shouting at me. My only consolation was that I wasn't wearing my Womble slippers. If you're going to be caught flat on your stomach in the middle of a car park after lights out, you should definitely be wearing state-of-the-art Reebok trainers.

I was in such a panic that it was a few seconds before I realized that, although someone was shouting, it wasn't Mr Palfry. It was Kuba Bamber. Lord knows how she got out of the girls' lodge and across the car park, but she was up on the porch of the boys' lodge. Mr Palfry was trying to get past her, but Kuba was hanging on to him and begging him to come and help Mrs Smiley, while at the same time blocking the door and making it impossible for him to move.

"Ariel saw a ghost!" Kuba was gibbering excitedly. "It's true, Mr Palfry. A real ghost. Two ghosts, in fact." Her voice got even louder. "One was just a blob of ectoplasm, glowing and sort of floating along the ground. And the other was a Roman soldier."

Mr Palfry had to struggle to get a word in. "Calm down, Kuba," he kept shouting. "Just calm down."

In the main room of the girls' lodge, Mrs Smiley was having a similar conversation with Ariel.

"They're in the car park!" howled Ariel. "Ghosts, Mrs Smiley. I saw them with my own eyes!"

Mrs Smiley wasn't as mellow as Mr Palfry. "For heaven's sake, be quiet, Ariel!" she ordered. "I can't hear myself think!"

Since I was still in the car park, I knew there weren't any ghosts, but I did see something.

There were two figures hovering round the corner of the girls' lodge. Eddie and Mark had managed to escape after depositing Archie, but because they were at the side of the building, they couldn't make a run for it without being seen by Mr Palfry.

Unlike me. Kuba was nearly as tall as Mr Palfry and, standing in front of him as she was, she totally kept me from his sight.

"Kuba!" Mr Palfry shouted wearily. "Kuba, if you'd just get out of my way…"

It was my only chance. As I turned and ran, Mrs Smiley's voice rang through the night once more.

"Good grief, Archie!" it said. "What on earth are you doing *there*?"

Like a soldier with only two minutes left to find and defuse the bomb, I raced round the lodge and in through the kitchen window. I was streaking up the stairs as Mr Palfry, Kuba still clinging to him, finally made it off the porch. I scrambled into bed and had just pulled the covers over me when the door opened and Mark and Eddie hurled themselves into the room and into their beds.

The door opened again and Mark and Eddie started snoring.

Mr Bombay counted softly. "One … two … three…"

There were a few minutes of silence after Mr Bombay shut our door and moved on down the hall and then Eddie and Mark both sat up.

"Foiled again," said Eddie. "I can't believe it. It was a perfect plan. The way Spongo sleeps he wouldn't have woken up until they all came down for breakfast." He sounded pretty disgruntled.

Mark sighed. "Boy, was that close," he whispered. "What was Ariel doing up, anyway? It would've worked if she hadn't gone off like a car alarm."

"Well, she won't be there on the walk tomorrow," answered Eddie. "She's in Mr Palfry's group and we're with Ms Kaye."

"That's right," said Mark. "We'll have Archie all to ourselves."

Eddie gave an evil chuckle. "In space, no one can hear a Spongo scream…"

THE EDUCATIONAL PART OF OUR TRIP BEGINS

Eddie and Mark, of course, were full of shock, amazement and surprise the next morning when Archie told them what had happened to him during the night.

"Mrs Smiley wouldn't believe that I didn't know how I got into the girls' lodge," Archie finished. "She was really angry." His eyes darted to the door of our room as though he expected one of the teachers to burst in, shouting at him. It was ironic that Archie was the only one of us who hadn't actually done anything, and he was the only one to get into trouble. "Mr Palfry too," he continued glumly. "I think Mr Palfry is thinking I'm strange."

Eddie laughed good-naturedly. "You are strange." He punched Archie in the arm, so he'd know this was just a joke between mates. "But you're still our friend."

"Yep," agreed Mark. "You're still our friend."

"I imagine I was walking in my sleep," said Archie. He looked from Eddie to Mark, and then to me. "But none of you heard me get up?"

Eddie shook his head regretfully. "I was so tired, I didn't hear a thing."

"Me neither," said Mark.

I said I'd slept through it all too. "Must be the mountain air," I said. "It knocked me out."

You may think this was me being a jelly again, but it wasn't. I knew I was lucky that Ariel and Kuba had distracted Mr Palfry and Mrs Smiley. I also knew I was lucky to have made it back to the room without Mark and Eddie seeing me. But since both those things had happened and everybody believed I really had slept through the whole thing, I was going to let them go on believing it. I reckoned it was what a shrewd businessman like Bill Gates would do. It gave me an advantage – and I needed an advantage if I was going to help Archie. Which was what I was going to do. I didn't feel I had a choice any more.

Eddie put a hand on Archie's shoulder. "Don't worry about Mr Palfry," said Eddie. "You stick with us, and you'll be fine."

"Yeah," said Mark. "You stick with us."

I didn't say anything. I reckoned I had my work cut out for me.

*   *   *

After breakfast, Mr Palfry discussed what we'd be doing for the next few days. Our official reason for the trip was to explore the woods and mountains and see how many different plants, animals, insects and birds we could find. We'd been divided into four groups (A, B, C and D), each with its own trail and a teacher to make sure no one fell over a cliff. Mr Palfry emphasized the importance of getting on with the members of our group.

"You're a team," said Mr Palfry. "You work together, and each of you is responsible for the others."

Archie and I were in group C with Eddie and Mark and two other boys. Eddie and Mark were deliriously happy about being with Ms Kaye. Ms Kaye was a pushover. The only thing that would have fitted in better with their plans would have been to have no teacher along at all. I looked over at Archie. He was smiling away, as though being put with a teacher who couldn't control a blade of grass, never mind Eddie Kilgour and Mark Crother, was the best news he'd had in his life. I stifled a sigh. It was my mother's fault. Being brought up by a woman with so many principles wasn't easy. She would never forgive me if anything happened to Archie, and neither would I.

Mr Palfry must suddenly have realized that

Ms Kaye was a pushover too. He looked at his clipboard, and then he looked at the four of us, and then he looked at Ms Kaye. He chewed on his lower lip in a thoughtful way.

"I think we'll make a slight change in group C," said Mr Palfry. "I think Archie, Elmo, Mark and Eddie had better come with me." He looked down at the angelic face of Kuba Bamber, who was sitting directly in front of him, apparently mesmerized by his words. "You and Ariel will stay in my group," he told her. "You'll be a calming influence on the boys."

I looked over at Kuba. She was smiling serenely at Mr Palfry, but she must have felt my eyes on her because she turned her head and gave me a wink.

And that's when I finally realized that luck had had nothing to do with Ariel's ghosts any more than luck had put her and Kuba in Mr Palfry's group.

So much for the promises of angels.

Eddie and Mark were the most athletic of our group, so they took the lead.

"Don't get too far ahead," warned Mr Palfry.

"We won't," Eddie promised.

"We've got our maps," said Mark.

It was difficult to tell whether or not Mr Palfry found this reassuring. He pointed to his

own map. "This is where we'll stop for lunch."
He drew a cross by the squiggle of lines that
marked a large pile of rocks. "It's called the
Sentry Stones. You can't miss it."

"Don't worry," said Eddie. "If we do get
ahead, we'll wait for you there."

They set off at a brisk pace, Archie trotting
behind them with their water and lunches in
his rucksack.

The rest of us fell into step behind them.

I knew I should try to keep up, but I was
hoping for a chance to talk to Kuba alone. I
had another piece of my mind to give her.

It wasn't long before I had my chance.
Eddie, Mark and Archie got well ahead
because they never stopped to take any notes,
and Mr Palfry and Ariel fell well behind
because Ariel's new pink hiking boots turned
out to be smaller than they'd been in the shop
and were slowing her down.

As soon as I was sure no one else could hear
us, I said, "I thought you weren't going to
interfere any more. I thought you promised."

Kuba looked offended. "Is that all the
thanks I get for sounding the alarm last
night?" she demanded. "Eddie and Mark were
already climbing out of the kitchen window of
our lodge by the time you were halfway across
the car park. If Ariel hadn't screamed they
would have seen you." She stopped to
watch Archie follow Mark and Eddie over

the nearest hill. "I couldn't let that happen, could I?"

I decided to change the subject.

"And what was all that stuff about ecto-plasm? I can understand making up the Roman soldier, but the ectoplasm was a bit much."

Kuba's eyes were focused on the distance. "I didn't make anything up," she informed me. "The ectoplasm was a glowing blob on the ground." She turned and pointed at my feet. "About that high, and shining."

If you think that angels can't sneer, let me tell you now that you're wrong.

Without even glancing at my new trainers I could see the glow-in-the-dark trim and inset; and I could see myself creeping through the dark, thinking I was invisible when I was actually shining like a torch.

"And what about the Roman soldier? Are you saying you didn't make him up either?"

"Of course I didn't," said Kuba, as though this was a ridiculous question. "Mrs Smiley doesn't believe it, but Ariel definitely saw a Roman soldier."

"In the car park?"

"That's right." She was ahead of me again, but she looked over her shoulder. Her smile flickered like a candle flame. "He was follow-ing the ectoplasm."

"Excuse me," I said, scrambling after her.

"But he wasn't following *me*. I think I would have noticed."

"Maybe." Kuba shrugged. "But I know for certain that Ariel wasn't half asleep, because I woke her up."

"You did?"

Kuba skipped on ahead of me. She obviously considered my question beneath even me, because she didn't bother to answer it. "So what are you planning to do about Eddie and Mark?" she asked over her shoulder.

I scrabbled up after her. "I don't know. Just keep an eye on them, I suppose."

"Oh, look!" Kuba stopped to peer down at a small plant growing between the rocks. "A Calipher's Star. That's really rare."

I was still cross. "You know, it's difficult for me to keep an eye on the others when you keep stopping all the time."

"It doesn't matter," said Kuba. "Let them get ahead. You're going to need the element of surprise."

"I am?" I huffed and puffed my way up beside her. "And am I allowed to ask why?"

In answer, Kuba plopped herself down on the nearest large rock. "We'd better wait for Mr Palfry and Ariel here. This is where we're meant to stop for lunch."

I looked over. To our left was a pile of rocks that hung over the valley as if they were watching what was going on. The Sentry Stones.

"Hang on a second," I protested. "What about Eddie, Archie and Mark?"

"They've gone," said Kuba.

I stood there, waiting for some more information. None came. Kuba took her notebook from her pocket and started sketching the Calipher's Star.

"Excuse me," I said, "but I'm waiting for an explanation. What do you mean they've gone? Gone from Wales? Gone from the planet?"

"Gone from the trail. They're getting Archie lost."

Kuba glanced behind her. Mr Palfry and Ariel had stopped far below us. Ariel had taken her shoes off and was rubbing her feet. Mr Palfry was wiping his forehead with the sleeve of his shirt.

I sank down beside her. "Lost?"

"In space, no one can hear you scream," mimicked Kuba. She handed me her notebook.

"What's this?'

"Look," she ordered.

I looked. At first all I saw was her sketch, but then an image began to appear over it, faintly at first, and then stronger and stronger.

"It's Mark and Eddie." I don't know why I was whispering; it wasn't as if they could hear me. "But where's Archie?"

"He's coming." Kuba leaned her head next to mine so she could see what was happening too. "See – there he is."

There he was. Eddie and Mark were waiting for Archie at the top of a hill, and Archie was struggling towards them, gasping under the weight of his rucksack.

"Be careful, Archie!" called Eddie. "Don't forget you've got our lunches. If you lose them, we'll have to eat *you*."

Archie smiled. "I can't see the others," he said as he staggered to a stop. "Have we left the trail?"

"Of course we haven't." Eddie got to his feet and stretched. "They're down there. Behind those trees."

Mark stood up too.

"We'd better push on," said Eddie. "It's not that far to the place we're meant to stop for lunch. We can wait for them there."

There was a stream on the other side of the hill. It wasn't exactly the Amazon River, but it was too deep to walk through and too wide to jump. There was an old tree trunk stretched across it that almost reached the other side.

Eddie crossed first.

"You next, Archie!" called Eddie. He stretched out his arm. "Grab hold and I'll help you across."

Archie took a deep breath and started inching his way to the other side, trying to balance the unwieldy rucksack.

Mark was behind him.

Mark flapped his arms in the air. "Geez, this is really slippery…" he cried as the log wobbled dangerously.

"Be careful!" Archie sounded a bit panicky. "You're going to make us fall."

"Now what?" I asked. "Are they going to drown him?"

"Not on purpose," said Kuba. She took her sandwich out of her bag and gave me half.

"Just grab hold of me!" ordered Eddie. He was still stretching towards Archie, but wasn't any closer to his hand than he had been when he started.

"I'm coming…" Archie took another cautious step. The log wobbled again. "I'm coming."

Mark said, "Oops!" and then the log really started rolling.

Archie made a grab for Eddie's hand.

"Oops, indeed," said Kuba as Archie fell in the water.

"Don't get the rucksack wet," Eddie shouted. "You'll ruin the sandwiches."

Mark was back on the other side, helpless with laughter.

"Why is Archie just lying there like an overturned tortoise?" I asked. "Why doesn't he get up?"

"He can't," said Kuba through a mouthful of cheese and pickle. "The rucksack's full of stones. He can't get the leverage."

"Help me!" called Archie. "I can't get up."

Mark had a simple suggestion. "Why don't we just leave him?"

Eddie considered this in silence.

Archie gave a little, nervous laugh. "Stop messing around! Help me up!"

"Maybe we should leave him," said Eddie thoughtfully. "It would be scientifically interesting to see how long it takes him to get up on his own."

"Nah, I've changed my mind," said Mark. "I want my lunch."

"Me too." Eddie grinned. "I'm starving." He pointed above them. "We'll go to that ridge and eat there."

Kuba and I watched them haul Archie out of the stream and climb up to the ridge in silence. As soon as they sat down, Eddie grabbed the rucksack from Archie and opened it up. He took out two sandwiches and handed them to Mark. Then he took two more out, and handed them to himself. He passed the bag back to Archie.

Archie was wet but smiling as he looked into the bag. He was still smiling when he looked back at Eddie. "There aren't any more sandwiches," said Archie.

I reckoned Eddie said something like "Oh, aren't there?" but it was hard to tell because his mouth was full.

"No, there aren't."

Mark started choking, but Eddie remained cool. "Are you sure you didn't drop them?" he asked.

"I'm very sure," said Archie.

Mark regained enough speech to say, "Maybe when you fell in the stream..."

"There's fruit," said the ever-generous Eddie Kilgour. "You can have that."

Still smiling, Archie started rummaging in the bag for the fruit. Kuba, of course, was right about the stones. Archie came up with two whose only relationship to food was that they were about the size of grapefruits.

That's when Archie finally understood the awful truth. He stopped smiling. I was afraid he was going to cry again.

I pushed the notebook away. "I think I've seen enough."

"Not quite." Kuba pushed it back.

Eddie and Mark were rolling about in fits of hysterics. Archie was dumping out the stones. When he had finished, he picked up the pack and got to his feet.

"I'm going on my own," he announced with as much dignity as someone who's just been made a complete fool of can. "From now on I'm a team of one."

This news upset Mark and Eddie about as much as you'd expect.

Archie stomped off without looking back.

When he vanished from the page I looked

up. "Now what do we do?" I asked.

"Don't look at me," said Kuba. "You don't want me to interfere, remember?"

WAR AT WYNDACH

I reckoned it was important to get Archie back as soon as possible. Archie was the one who had gone off on his own, so he was the one who was going to get in trouble. Again. I just didn't know how I planned to do it.

I looked below us. Ariel was putting her shoes back on. "What about Mr Palfry?" I asked.

"Ariel will keep him busy for a while longer," Kuba assured me.

"Ariel? Ariel's keeping him busy?"

"She's not stupid, you know," said Kuba with just a touch of self-righteousness. "Ariel saw Mark and Eddie as well as the ghosts, and pretty much worked out what was going on." She smiled rather smugly for someone with celestial connections. "She was only too happy to help. I reckon Mr Palfry will be so worn out by now that he won't ask too many questions.

I'll tell him you and the others finished your lunches and went off exploring." She gave me another smile. "So don't be too long. Eddie and Mark should be turning up soon."

Don't be too long? I didn't even know where I was going.

"But what if I don't find Archie?" This struck me as a rather important point. After all, it was a big mountain.

"You'll find him," Kuba assured me. "He won't have gone far. Try near the stream."

The route Mark and Eddie had taken ran more or less parallel to the route they were meant to take. Armed with my map, I found the stream without any trouble. I was pretty pleased. I didn't think a trained soldier could have done any better.

There was no one on the ridge now, though.

"Archie!" I called. "Archie! It's Elmo. Come on out!"

No answer echoed through the trees.

"Archie!" I called again. "Archie. It's me. You've got to come back."

I looked round, trying to think like someone who is angry and humiliated and doesn't know what he's doing or where he's going. It wasn't that difficult. I had quite a bit of personal experience to draw on. The day of the Womble slippers incident, I'd hidden in the teachers' toilet.

Hiding in the woods was different, though.

I'd known that if I hid in the teachers' toilet, someone would find me eventually. But if you hid in the woods, no one would have any idea where you were. Before Archie could really go off in a sulk, he'd have to make sure that Mr Palfry knew that was what he was doing. So I reasoned that Archie would be looking for the rest of us, and was probably going back the way he'd come.

I headed downstream.

For a while the trail was narrow, and hemmed in by particularly spiky indigenous trees, but then it got so narrow that I couldn't actually see it any more.

I took the map out again, and looked for some sort of landmark. The stream was a tiny dotted line that didn't seem to pass anything of geographical significance.

"Archie!" I shouted. "Archie! It's Elmo! Please come out!"

The only answer was the chatter of the birds.

I stood dead still, watching and listening for some movement or sound that might be Archie, but there was none – unless he'd suddenly sprouted wings.

I groaned.

Maybe I shouldn't have made such a big deal about Kuba interfering – I could have done with her notebook. And then I thought of Bill Gates. Bill Gates never gave up, and I was pretty sure he had never had any help from an angel. If Bill Gates could keep going in the face of defeat, then I could too.

Determined, I stood up tall (well, as tall as I could) and lifted my chin. That's when I saw something move in the woods ahead of me that was too large to be an indigenous mammal or bird. Whatever it was, it was pretty far away, and the woods were dense, so I couldn't say that it was definitely Archie, but it was on its own, human, the right size, and it was carrying something in its arms that looked like a rucksack to me.

"Archie!" I shouted. "Archie, wait!"

He didn't wait, of course. He was angry, humiliated and confused, a condition that can make you forget your manners. I'd only come out of the toilet on the day of the Womble slippers because the caretaker threatened to take the door off its hinges if I didn't.

I ran after the distant figure.

"Archie, stop!" I called. "It's me, Elmo! Everything's going to be all right! I've come to take you back."

But Archie still didn't stop. Instead, he quickened his pace and marched deeper into the woods.

I reckoned I was getting the hang of being a soldier, because I didn't even think twice about following. Using my arm as a shield, I fought my way through the thickest trees. It didn't even bother me that my Nike sweatshirt was being clawed at by branches and my new trainers were being covered with mud and leaf mould, that's how determined I was. I'd show Kuba Bamber I didn't need her help.

I finally caught up with him, but not because of my skills as a tracker. He was sitting on a log in a small clearing, waiting for me.

Only it wasn't Archie.

It was a small, swarthy man with a spear and a shield in his hands. He got up as I bashed my way into the clearing. And then he disappeared, just like a bubble.

"Archie!" I screamed. "Where are you?"

"Elmo?" Archie's voice was so low, I wasn't sure if I'd really heard it or not.

"Archie?"

This time his voice was a bit stronger. "Elmo, is that you?"

"Archie!" I nearly tripped in my excitement. "I've been looking everywhere for you!"

There was a crackle behind me. Archie was stepping out of the cave-like hollow in an enormous old tree where he'd been hiding.

"Kuba and I got worried when you didn't turn up at the Sentry Stones," I lied. "What happened?"

"It's a long story," said Archie.

I sat down on a dead trunk. "That's OK," I said. "I've got time."

*   *   *

93

Standing a lot straighter than most of the trees around us, and staring at the ground all the time, Archie told me what had happened.

I knew most of it already, of course, but I pretended to be shocked and surprised. "You're joking!"

"It's all true," said Archie. "I would not be surprised if it was Mark and Eddie who put me in the girls' lodge last night."

"What creeps!" I shook my head in amazement. "We'd better go back and sort them out."

Archie frowned. "I appreciate you coming for me, Elmo," he solemnly told me, "but I'm not going back."

To tell you the truth, that wasn't the response I'd been expecting.

"What do you mean, you're not going back? You can't stay here. You've got to go back."

"No, I haven't."

I'd never suspected there was a stubborn side to Archie Spongo before but it was out now, in full force.

"Let Eddie and Mark get in trouble for a change," he went on. He didn't sound much like his usual, meek self. "Let them get in trouble for losing me. That's what they deserve."

"They deserve a lot more than that," I said. "But they didn't lose you. *You* ran away."

Archie sat down beside me. "It adds up to the same thing."

"No, it doesn't," I argued. "Eddie and Mark will tell some story about you getting all weird and stomping off, and it'll be their word against yours."

Archie shook his head. Stubbornly. "But they'll be in trouble when Mrs Smiley and Mr Palfry hear the truth," he insisted.

"And what's the truth?" I asked. "That you fell off a log? That you were too stupid to realize that a few sandwiches shouldn't weigh several kilos?"

Archie glared at me. "I'm staying here till Mr Palfry finds me."

"And what will that solve?" I asked him.

"It solves the problem of how I survive the next few days, that's what it solves. If Mr Palfry has to search for me, the trip will most likely be cancelled after that."

Arguing with Archie was a lot like arguing with myself. I almost knew what he was going to say before he said it.

"And then?" I persisted. "Then what happens?"

"Then we go home."

"Right," I agreed. "And then everything's just the same as it was – or maybe worse. Things only get worse if you don't stand up for what's right."

That was something I'd learned from the incident with Mr Bamber and his bulldozers, only I'd sort of forgotten it in all my excitement about being famous, and getting my sweatshirt, and everything.

"I don't care," said Archie. "I just want to go home."

"You can't go home." I handed him a tissue. "This isn't over yet."

"It's over for me," said Archie. "Eddie and Mark will tell everybody what happened. They'll all be laughing at me."

"Who cares?" I said. I handed him a sandwich and the apple from my own lunch. "It doesn't matter what *they* do, it only matters what *you* do." It sounded like something Grace Blue, or even Kuba Bamber, might say, but it also sounded true.

Either Archie thought so too, or the food was improving his mood, because I could tell from the way he was listening that he was starting to weaken.

"Don't you understand?" It was as though I was on automatic pilot; the words came steaming out. "If you don't stand up to Eddie and Mark, they'll keep pushing you around. Right?"

Archie nodded. "Correct."

"But if you do stand up to them—"

"They'll keep pushing me around," finished Archie.

"Well, maybe... But even if they do, it's different because you're not just letting them do it to you. As long as you don't fight back, you're telling them it's all right."

Archie looked at the sandwich he was holding for a couple of seconds, and then he looked over at me. "Do you really believe that?"

"Yes," I said. Considering the way I'd been acting myself, I was a bit surprised to realize this was true. "Yes, I do."

"All right." Archie sighed. "We'll go back and tell Mr Palfry what they did."

But I was feeling bold and inspired. I wanted us to sort this out ourselves.

"No." I shook my head. "No, we'll go back, but we'll carry on as though nothing has happened."

"Are you serious?" said Archie.

"There's an old saying in English that it might be useful for you to know," I told him.

Archie regarded me warily. "What is it?"

"He who laughs last, laughs longest."

LAUGHING LAST

Eddie and Mark must have arrived at the Sentry Stones just before us, because Mr Palfry was still telling them off when we got there.

"What do you mean, you don't know where Archie and Elmo are?" he was saying. "Kuba said the four of you went off exploring together after lunch."

Eddie Kilgour at a loss for words was a rare sight. I found it pretty enjoyable.

"Well – uh…" said Eddie. He glanced over at Kuba, who was smiling at him as if he was the baby in the manger. "Yeah, we did." It was obvious he had no idea why she was lying. "But – uh – then we split up."

"Yeah." Mark nodded. "Then we split up."

I gave Archie a nudge.

"Here we are!" he called out.

Ariel and Kuba were examining Ariel's new shoes and didn't look up, but the other three turned as though their heads were controlled by the same string.

"We found some – uh – some Calipher's Stars," I said to Mr Palfry. "That's what took us so long. It took us a while to sketch them."

"It's all right," said Mr Palfry, glancing at Ariel. "It's not as if we're in a hurry." He gave a little laugh. "I didn't get worried till the boys said they didn't know where you were."

"We split up," I said. "We told them we'd meet them back here." I grinned at Eddie and Mark. "Isn't that what we agreed?"

Mark said, "Yeah."

Eddie just looked at me.

"Right then," said Mr Palfry. "Now, how are those feet of yours, Ariel? Think you can do some more walking?"

"She'll be fine," said Kuba. "I think we've solved the problem."

I continued to grin at Eddie and Mark. I reckoned I'd solved the problem too.

The rest of the day was eventful only from a scientific or botanical perspective. We spotted a variety of flora and fauna, including quite a few Calipher's Stars.

"This is remarkable," Mr Palfry kept saying every time Kuba found another. "I thought Calipher's Stars were rarer than hens' teeth."

"Oh, no," said Kuba. "I don't think they're that rare."

There was no more trouble from Eddie and Mark. In fact, there was no more communication between us of any sort. They abandoned their pretence of being mates with Archie, and kept their distance from the rest of us. But they watched. Every time I looked up from admiring some insect or leaf, I'd catch one of them just turning away. They were suspicious, and they were cautious. I reckoned we had them on the run.

"I wouldn't start congratulating yourself too soon," said Kuba at supper that night. "They're probably just biding their time."

"She's right," said Archie morosely. "They're waiting until they get us alone."

"So what?" I asked with slightly more confidence than I felt. Now that we were back in civilization I was feeling less like a soldier and more like a twelve-year-old boy with a dark past again. "They're not going to beat us up, are they?"

"In room 3B, no one can hear you scream..." whispered Kuba.

I knew she was joking, but I didn't feel like laughing. I wished I hadn't said anything about not interfering. She could interfere all she wanted – it seemed likely that we'd need the help.

Kuba laughed. "You know, Elmo," she said. "There's another old saying in English that it might be good for you to know."

Archie blinked, obviously surprised that she was saying to me exactly what I had said to him, but I just stared back at her blankly.

"And what's that?" I asked.

"God helps those who help themselves," said Kuba.

As soon as the door of our room shut behind us that night, Eddie and Mark put an end to the awful suspense of wondering what they would do next.

They'd obviously made a full recovery from their bewilderment of the afternoon.

"Hey, Elmo!" Eddie blocked me as I tried to get to my bed. "Just what do you think you were doing today? Who told you to mess around in our business?"

"Yeah," said Mark. "Who told you to mess around in our business?"

Archie stepped up beside me. Like most people, he's a lot taller than I am, which was something of a comfort. "Leave Elmo alone," he ordered. "He hasn't done anything to you."

"Well, maybe I think he has." Eddie leered. "But don't feel left out, Spongo, 'cause we'll deal with you later."

I pulled myself up to my full height, which just about reached the shoulders of the others.

"I have absolutely no idea what you're talking about." I smiled calmly. "Archie and I went exploring after lunch, just like you two. Remember?"

But Mr Palfry wasn't with us now.

"No," said Eddie. "I don't remember. What I remember is you and Kuba being miles behind us, and the next thing I know you're skipping back with Spongo here, yammering about finding some plant."

I squeezed past him. "If you'll excuse me, I'd like to go to bed now." I threw myself on my bunk.

"Why didn't you two squeal to Mr Palfry?" asked Mark. He gave Archie a disdainful look. "And why aren't you crying like you usually do?"

Archie didn't flinch. "Crying?" he said. "What have I got to cry about?"

Mark took a step towards him. "I'll give you something to cry about," he promised.

Eddie laughed. "Just wait till tomorrow. Both of you will be crying. And you won't be crying tears, you'll be crying waterfalls."

"That's right," chimed in Mark. "We've got some great things planned for you two."

"We cannot wait," said Archie. "Can we, Elmo?"

I started pulling down my covers. "No," I agreed. "I'm quivering with anticipation."

"That's not anticipation," said Mark. "That's fear. Cluckcluckcluckcluckcluck…"

Eddie leaned over me so that I could feel his hot breath on my ear. "This isn't over yet, you know," he informed me in the calm and pleasant voice of a serial killer. "It's just begun."

I sat up, my back against the wall. Archie had started to get into his own bunk, but he changed his mind and stood by mine. He was looking a bit nervous. I forced myself to stay cool and calm.

"If I were you I'd call my mummy now and ask her to come and take me home," said Mark. "Before you embarrass yourselves in front of everybody."

"You mean like waking up in the girls' lodge in my pyjamas?" asked Archie.

"Oooh..." shrieked Eddie. "Look who found a brain."

I smiled coldly. "Well, it wasn't either of you, that's for certain."

That cracked them up. They punched each other and honked with glee.

Archie had to get up on the ladder to avoid being trampled on.

Which is why I saw the soldiers first. I was watching Eddie and Mark dancing around like Rumpelstiltskin when he thinks the Queen can't guess his name, and then, out of the corner of my eye, I saw something shimmer near the foot of my bed.

I glanced over. Six small but sturdy men were coming through the outside wall.

"Archie!" I hissed. "Archie! Look!"

Archie leaned down to peer into my bunk. I

pointed towards the wall. "There!" I whispered. "Look there!"

We both turned our heads for a clearer view. The six soldiers wore helmets and breastplates and what looked like grubby skirts. Two of them had shields, and all of them had knives and spears. The one in the lead was the same man I'd seen in the woods that afternoon. They came to a halt at the foot of the beds and closed ranks. Except for the leader, they looked a bit confused.

"I don't know what you two think you're up to," Eddie was saying. "But if you want a war, we'll be happy to give you one."

It wasn't easy to concentrate with the soldiers hovering at the foot of the bunk, but I managed to answer. "We don't want a war," I said. "We just want you two to stop acting like geeks."

"Don't you ever look in the mirror?" sneered Eddie. "*You're* the geek."

"I think there is something *you* should look at," said Archie.

Eddie put on a horrified face. "Don't tell me," he said. "There's one of Ariel's ghosts behind me."

"Is it wearing pink ribbons?" asked Mark.

"No," I said, "they're not. They're armed."

"I believe they must belong to the Roman army," put in Archie.

This was almost too funny for our room-mates to bear. They clutched at each other, helpless with hilarity.

The soldiers marched forward, spears held straight. They kept marching when they got to Eddie and Mark, and went right through them like a cloud. Then they turned round and went back to where they'd been. One of the soldiers passed a hand through Eddie's head while his comrades watched with worried expressions. They obviously weren't expecting us any more than we were expecting them. Except for the leader, that was. He'd picked up my trainers from the floor and was studying them intently.

"Roman soldiers!" gasped Eddie, oblivious to the men hulking around him. "Don't you ever give up, Elmo?"

I was pretty chuffed to be able to say, "No, I suppose I don't."

Unafraid of Eddie and Mark choking and spluttering in their T-shirts and shorts, the soldiers made a circle around them and studied them with curiosity and concern.

"We're telling you, there are six Roman soldiers standing round you," said Archie. "I really think you should take a look."

One of the soldiers broke away from the others and went over to the chest of drawers.

"Oh, right," Eddie chortled. "We're really scared." He pretended to shake with fear. "What are we going to do, Mark? Six big, tough Roman soldiers—"

"They're not that big," I corrected. "But they do look tough. Only now it isn't six, it's five."

"Oh, now it's five," Eddie mimicked.

"What he means," cut in Archie, "is that there are six altogether, but one of them is over by the chest of drawers now."

"Why?" joked Mark. "Did he forget his socks?"

I was about to say that it looked as if he was going to borrow some when one of the drawers suddenly slid open. The soldier slowly reached in and pulled out Eddie's discman. You could tell that he was saying something because his lips moved as he glanced over his shoulder, but he didn't make a sound. The other soldiers all looked at him, their lips moving, but they made no sound either. The soldier turned the discman this way and that, while his comrades watched. He shook it. He tapped it. He looked over at his mates again and shrugged. He couldn't make out what it was. Advanced technology for him was the wheel.

I smiled at Mark. "No, he didn't forget his socks. I think he's interested in your music."

Mark rubbed the tears from his eyes with his T-shirt. "I don't care if Mr Palfry gives me detentions for the rest of my life," he said. "I've got to tell everybody. They're not going to believe this one."

It didn't seem that Roman soldiers were chosen for their patience. Giving up on his efforts to make out what it was he was holding, the soldier said something and tossed the discman to another soldier, who raised a hand to catch it. Unlike the soldiers themselves, however, the discman didn't go through Eddie. It hit him on the shoulder.

That caught his attention. It caught Mark's attention too.

The two of them finally looked round.

The soldiers stared back. They were a long way from Rome, and had seen many strange things, but their expressions suggested that we were the strangest.

Eddie's eyes shifted warily, but otherwise he was as motionless as a mountain. "What is this?" he asked. I'd never heard his voice so soft. "Some kind of joke?"

Mark was looking pretty wary too. "I know what it is," he said, his eyes on the spear of the soldier who was sniffing at him now. "They're projecting a film into the room from outside."

"Of course we are," said Archie. "We've plugged it into a tree."

I laughed. I'd never realized what a good sense of humour Archie had before.

Archie laughed too, but Mark flinched as one of the soldiers moved closer to inspect his earring.

"Eddie..." said Mark. "Eddie... If it isn't a

trick, what do you think it is?"

Eddie licked his lips, but he didn't say anything. I could understand why. One of the soldiers was trying to unlace his trainers with the tip of a spear. It was a pretty gripping sight.

"Well, we know they can't be ghosts, right?" whispered Mark.

Eddie made a rattling sound, which I took to be his new way of laughing.

"Of course they're not ghosts." He was trying to bluster, but it came out more like a bleat. "There's no such thing as ghosts."

"Maybe you should get Mr Palfry," suggested Archie.

If Eddie or Mark found anything ironic in that suggestion, they didn't show it. They acted as if getting Mr Palfry was the best idea they'd ever heard. Only neither of them moved. They couldn't without walking through a man with a shield.

"I'll get him," I volunteered. I looked up at Archie. "D'you want to come with me?"

Archie grinned. "Yes. I know the way well."

I was just getting out of my bunk when the stillness of the mountain night was smashed into about a zillion pieces by a shrill, almost unearthly shrieking.

Mark and Eddie grabbed hold of one another, as though a mob of banshees might be running about outside.

"Now what?" one of them whispered.

The lights went on in the porch of the lodge across the way. Footsteps sounded in the corridor outside our door.

The soldiers were distracted by the wailing too. They moved their mouths at one another and then, raising their shields and their swords, they ran to the window.

"Hey, hang on a minute!" I shouted. The lead soldier had my new trainers on his feet. "My shoes!"

He turned round and pointed to the floor at the side of the bed. I looked down. There was a small plant in a handmade pot sitting where my trainers used to be.

I looked back at the soldier, but he was following the others through the wall and out into the night.

By now it sounded like we really were in a disaster film. All the outside lights had been turned on and the shrieking was out of control. I could hear the teachers shouting, "Calm down! Calm down!"

Mark and Eddie were too traumatized to do more than stand there, staring, but Archie was already climbing down to the floor.

"Come on," said Archie. "Let's see what's going on."

Kuba was sitting on the steps of the boys' lodge, watching the chaos only a few metres away as though she was watching television.

Archie ran straight down the stairs, but I sat

down beside her. I reckoned she already knew about the soldiers in our room, so I didn't start in about that. I gestured towards the girls' lodge. Mrs Smiley and Ms Kaye had all the girls in the main room. I could see them through the window. Mr Palfry and Mr Lewis, each armed with a torch, were creeping around outside, looking for intruders.

"What happened?" I asked.

"Ariel found a centurion trying on her Calvin Klein dressing gown," said Kuba. "It really upset her. How did your lot take the Roman legions?"

I laughed. "Pretty much as you'd expect." I wasn't sure if I should thank her or not. "So," I said. "You're not going to get in more trouble for this, are you?"

Kuba's eyes were the eyes of the just-born. "In trouble for what?"

"You know," I said. "For raising the dead again."

"Of course not." Kuba winked. "I didn't raise the dead."

"You didn't?"

Kuba shook her head. "Mr Palfry said there'd been a Roman fort here once." She shrugged. "I suppose we were caught in a time warp."

"A time warp..." I gave her an enquiring look. "So you had nothing to do with it?"

Kuba jumped to her feet. "I'd better get

back. Mrs Smiley will think I've been kid-napped or something."

I repeated, "So you had nothing to do with it?"

Kuba stared across the way. Just past the lodge I could make out several short, sturdy men marching towards the woods. One of them was wearing Reebok trainers that glowed in the dark. He turned and waved at Kuba. She waved back.

"What am I supposed to do with the plant he left?" I asked.

"Give it to your mother," said Kuba. "She'll love it. It's been extinct for two hundred years."

UNDERCOVER ANGEL
Dyan Sheldon

Twelve-year-old Elmo Blue admires his neighbours, the Bambers – they're so nice and normal. Not like Elmo's embarrassing mother, who is declaring war on Mr Bamber over his plans to turn the local woods into a golf course. Elmo pins his hopes of being normal on making friends with the Bambers' new adopted child, an orphan from South America. But when the kid arrives, claiming to be an undercover angel, Elmo realizes that in fact his life is going to become distinctly weirder!

"Another thoroughly good read from a reliably entertaining author." *Kids Out*

CONFESSIONS OF A TEENAGE DRAMA QUEEN
Dyan Sheldon

Everything I'm about to tell you occurred exactly as I say. And I don't just mean the stuff about "Deadwood" High, and my fight with Carla Santini over the school play. I mean *everything*. Even the things that seem so totally out of this solar system that you think I *must* have made them up – like crashing the party after Sidartha's farewell concert in New York – they're true too. And nothing's been exaggerated. Not the teeniest, most subatomic bit. It's all happened exactly as I'm telling it.

And it starts with the end of the world...

"An outrageously funny and fast-moving story." *The Northern Echo*

"Delicious reading... Home-grown drama queens and teen shrinking violets will love it." *Kids Out*

RIDE ON, SISTER VINCENT
Dyan Sheldon

"A miracle. That's what St Agnes really needs. A miracle, not a motor mechanic."

Sent to the dilapidated convent school, St Agnes in the Pasture, dynamic, globe-trotting Sister Vincent, teacher of motor mechanics, feels like a fish out of water.

Certainly Mother Margaret Aloysius, the nuns and the school's three young pupils consider her a bit of an odd fish.

The Lord, it seems, is moving in a very mysterious way indeed – until the discovery in the old barn enables Sister Vincent to give the rundown school a surprising and exhilarating kick-start!

TALL, THIN AND BLONDE
Dyan Sheldon

Torn between the weird and the glamorous, which way will Jenny go?

Best friends Jenny and Amy have no time for Miss Perfect Teenagers, the tall, thin blondes whose only talk is of boys and fashion. At least, they *didn't*. Now, suddenly Amy's changed: she's into salads and diet Cokes; she's got a new hairstyle, wardrobe and set of friends. Jenny, meanwhile, finds herself part of a group of oddballs nicknamed the Martians. Will she follow Amy or find her own way?

"The teenage girl's lot ... is treated with empathy and humour." *The Times Educational Supplement*

"Frequently hilarious." *The Irish Times*

THE BOY OF MY DREAMS
Dyan Sheldon

When will she meet Him, the guy, the one, the boy of her dreams?

Michelle (commonly known as Mike) just can't stop thinking about it. And then it happens. She meets Him. Bill. He's gorgeous. He's cool. He's in college. Mike thinks Bill is her destiny. Bill says they look good together. But Bone, Mike's oldest friend, thinks her hormones are really damaging her brain... Is this true love – or total lunacy?

"Very funny and spot on." *The Mail on Sunday*

STORMBREAKER
Anthony Horowitz

Meet Alex Rider, the reluctant teenage spy.

When his guardian dies in suspicious circumstances, fourteen-year-old Alex Rider finds his world turned upside down.

Within days he's gone from schoolboy to superspy. Forcibly recruited into MI6, Alex has to take part in gruelling SAS training exercises. Then, armed with his own special set of secret gadgets, he's off on his first mission.

His destination is the depths of Cornwall, where Middle-Eastern multi-millionaire Herod Sayle is producing his state-of-the-art Stormbreaker computers. Sayle's offered to give one free to every school in the country – but MI6 think there's more to the gift than meets the eye.

Only Alex can find out the truth. But time is running out and Alex soon finds himself in mortal danger. It looks as if his first assignment may well be his last…

Explosive, thrilling, action-packed, *Stormbreaker* reveals Anthony Horowitz at his brilliant best.

BURGER WUSS
M.T. Anderson

Anthony is a wuss ... until the day he finds his girlfriend in someone else's arms!

Then Anthony vows revenge and devises The Plan. It begins with getting a job at O'Dermott's, the burger restaurant where Turner (aka *the guy who stole his girlfriend*) happens to be a star employee. It involves one anarchist, one condiment troll and one '85 Oldsmobile named Margot. But will Anthony's hunger for revenge be satisfied? And will he ever prove he's not a wuss?

Burger Wuss is a deliciously piquant story of love and betrayal, with a side order of retribution – served up with comic relish!

DANDELION AND BOBCAT
Veronica Bennett

Bobcat doesn't want a foster-sister – especially not one like Dandelion…

Not only does she have the weirdest looks he's ever seen, but she tells all his classmates that her real mother has been kidnapped! Bobcat doesn't know if she's lying or just plain nuts, but some unexplained events make him wonder if there is more to Dandelion than meets the eye. Why do her crazy predictions keep coming true? Who are her real parents? And do the answers lie in the mysterious Tarantula computer game?

Fast-paced, funny and sprinkled with magic, this is a hugely enjoyable story from the author of *Monkey*.